The Little

CW00525196

The Little Black Bottle

Choppy Warburton, the Question of Doping, and the
Deaths of His Bicycle Racers

Gerry Moore

Cycle Publishing / Van der Plas Publications, San Francisco

Copyright 2012, Cycle Publishing
Printed in the USA
2nd printing, revised, 2011

Published by:
Cycle Publishing / Van der Plas Publications)
1282 7th Avenue
San Francisco, CA 94122, USA
Tel: (415) 665-8214
Fax: (415) 753-8572
E-mail: con.tact@cyclepublishing.com
Web site: http://www.cyclepublishing.com

Distributed or represented to the book trade by:
USA: Midpoint Trade Books, New York, NY
Great Britain: Orca Book Services / Chris Lloyd Sales and Marketing
                Services, Poole, Dorset
Australia: Woodslane Pty Ltd, Warrieswood, NSW

Cover design: Cycle Design, San Francisco

Frontispiece: Jules Beau photograph showing Choppy Warburton,
                flanked by Arthur Linton (left), Jimmy Michael, and
                Tom Linton (far right)

Publisher's Cataloging in Publication Data
Moore, Gerry 1933–2010. The Little Black Bottle: Choppy Warburton, the
Question of Doping, and the Deaths of His Bicycle Racers
p. 22.6 cm. Includes bibliographic information and index
1. Bicycle Racing; 2. Sports History; 3. Doping
II. Title: Choppy Warburton, the Question of Doping, and the Deaths of His
Bicycle Racers
ISBN 978-1-892495-67-9 (paperback original)
Library of Congress Control Number 2011926709

About the Author

G ERRY MOORE (1933–2010) was born in Kensington, London. During the war years, his family lived in Garsington, Oxfordshire, where his father served as a butler. In his early teens, Gerry worked on the land, until at the age of 16 his family returned to London. At this time he discovered his love for cycling. He was a founding member of the Chequers Bicycle Club, which still exists today.

In his working life, Gerry was a draftsman/designer, which he carried out with great skill. He completed his National Service in the Royal Air Force, where he qualified as an Armourer and Sniper.

After his retirement, he moved to Weeting, in rural Norfolk, with his wife, Alma. There, due to the favourable terrain, his cycling interests were rekindled. Gerry had an intense interest in the cycling artist Frank Patterson. He wrote many articles and other publications about Patterson and his work.

In his later years, Gerry became a keen amateur cycling historian, spending many hours surfing the Internet for relevant information. He was also an avid collector of antique and unusual bicycles, and was happiest when sitting in his garden polishing and restoring antique bicycle parts.

Gerry passed away in January 2010, not yet knowing that his book would be published, shortly followed by his wife Alma. It has to be said that Gerry would not have been able to follow his interest in bikes so passionately without the ongoing support and dedication from Alma. He will be sorely missed by all who knew him.

Table of Contents

Introduction 7

Chapter 1. Introducing Choppy 9

Chapter 2. Choppy, the Coach 19

Chapter 3. About That Little Black Bottle 61

Chapter 4. "Champion Cyclist of the World" 68

Chapter 5. The Other Lintons. 93

Chapter 6. The Fearless "Boy Wonder" 107

Chapter 7. Choppy's Other Riders 141

Chapter 8. Other Trainers and Their Charges 151

Bibliography and Sources 168

Index 171

Introduction

IN THE LATE 1890s, Great Britain was still enjoying the advantages of the industrial revolution. The British Empire covered two-thirds of the world, Queen Victoria was on the throne as mother of the nation, and all was well in God's kingdom.

Well, not quite... The cursed English class system was firmly in place and pervaded all aspects of society—education, employment, medicine, the armed forces, and government. The upper class in their mansions owned most of the land. The middle class provided the doctors, lawyers, clergy, and commissioned ranks of the armed forces; they were educated in private schools and universities, well fed, and confident of their position in society. The remaining masses were the working class, who provided the labor to fuel industry, till the land, and fight the wars; they were poorly educated, underfed, underpaid, and housed in appalling conditions.

Although sport was enjoyed by all classes, it was generally conceived as an amateur pastime, administered by the middle classes. Professional sport was tolerated, but not encouraged. Administrators were forced to admit professionals into their organizations and to organize events for them, but they were strictly controlled and were not allowed to compete against amateurs. Against this background, there emerged an ever-increasing group of amateur sports people from the working class who were determined to use their natural abilities to improve their position in life by turning professional.

There were, of course, certain sports where professionalism was accepted without comment: pugilists from the days of bare knuckle fighting had accepted payment from their very first bout; stable lads who showed they had a talent for riding race horses progressed naturally into becoming paid jockeys, and athletics had a long tradition of professional runners, particularly in Scotland.

Cycling made a late entry into professionalism, and although there were races organized for boneshakers, ordinaries, and solid-tired safeties, and some high-wheel riders had accepted payment for competing, it was not until the introduction of the pneumatic-tired safety bicycle, around 1890, that a professional class of riders became firmly established.

By the late 1890s the controlling body for cycle racing in Britain was the National Cyclists Union (NCU). They had banned racing on the open road, thus closing that branch of competition to the British riders, whereas on the continent there were no such restrictive practices and road racing was promoted with vigor. Consequently, the best British riders turned to the track, and because of this specialization, became some of the best in the world, enjoying huge popularity.

This is the story of a group of young racing cyclists and their trainers who followed such a path. They came from humble backgrounds, were discovered by experienced trainer/managers, turned professional, and went on to become national and world champions.

Physical and mental breakdowns caused by unaccustomed wealth, public adoration, drugs, and alcohol is not something that only happens to present-day sports people.

Athletes and their managers in the late nineteenth century were under the same pressure to succeed: victory was everything, defeat meant oblivion. The sports stars of yesteryear were constantly in the public eye; every aspect of their lives was reported in newspapers worldwide. The constant travel and demands on their time played havoc with relationships and marriages. They all experienced joy, triumph, and defeat in equal measure. Some retired in comfort, while many others faced failure and an ignominious departure from the world.

Chapter 1.

Introducing Choppy

LATE IN THE MORNING of Friday the 17th December 1897, in a dingy back bedroom of a small nondescript terraced house in the northern suburbs of London, a man in late middle-age died of heart failure. It may seem an un-newsworthy event in an unremarkable part of the capital, yet the following day news of his death was telegraphed all over the world.

Who was this man lodging at 45 Sidney Road, Wood Green? His name was James Edward Warburton, the once famous—some would say infamous—long-distance runner and trainer of

Right: Fig. 1.1. Sorry, it's a rather poor-quality picture, but it's one of the few that show Choppy Warburton in his running days, leading an unidentified runner in front of a huge crowd.

world-class racing cyclists, known universally as "Choppy." He was born on the 13th November 1845; just two months after his parents married, in a three-storey house at Coal Hey, a district of Haslingden, a market town a few miles south of Accrington, Lancashire.

Haslingden was a typical Lancashire town, where practically the whole population worked in the local cotton mills and lived in streets of mean terraced houses, without running water and sanitation, with front doors opening directly onto the street, and with a yard at the back complete with bucket privy. It was said that when one worker complained to his employer, the mill owner, that the house he rented was not fit to live in, he was told, "the house wasn't for living in but for sleeping in; the mill was for living in." This incident explained perfectly the relationship that existed between employer and employee at that time.

Cotton mills dominated the town, with tall chimneys belching forth smoke and soot that combined with emissions from a thousand domestic coal fires, to cover the buildings and their inhabitants in grime. It made breathing difficult, and clothing almost impossible to wash clean. Men breathed in the filth and spat it out wherever they were, at home on the fire, and when in public on the pavement and in the gutters. Every pub supplied spittoons, so they could spit when they drank. Strangely it was only men that spat, never the women; perhaps the practice was considered manly. Bathing was restricted to a tin tub in front of the parlor fire once a week, so maintaining an acceptable standard of personal hygiene was a challenge that many a mill worker found impossible to attain.

Choppy was the eldest of thirteen children born to his parents James and Harriet. Being the first-born son, James was automatically given the family nickname of Choppy at birth, while his father became known as "Owed Choppy." At the time of his birth, his father was employed as a weaver in a cotton mill. Children from the families of mill workers were all expected to work to supplement the family income. They had worked a sixty-hour week until 1844, when an Act of Parliament halved the hours to allow children to attend school. Unfortunately, these restrictions were rarely adhered to, and in practice the children working at the mills received little education.

Young Warburton was put to work in a mill at just eight years of age, as he was small enough to crawl under the moving looms to collect loose cotton. So it was that he began his working life. A weaving shed in a cotton mill was an unpleasant and dangerous place. It was hot and dusty, and the looms created so much clatter that speech was impossible and the workers had to communicate by lip reading and hand signals. Later in life, Warburton was well known for his extravagant gestures when talking; perhaps this idiosyncrasy acquired in his youth carried over into adulthood.

As a youth, he was employed in various capacities at Carr and Bank Mills, owned by James Hey and John Duckwork. When he was about seventeen years of age, one of his duties was to go down to Helmshore railway station to instruct the station master to despatch an engine up the sidings to the mill to

Below: Fig. 1.2. Cotton mill in Choppy Warburton's birth place, Haslingden, Lancashire.

pull the loaded wagons up to the station and onto the mail line. Warburton had got into the habit of running alongside the locomotive all the way back to the mill. John Duckwork, who was not only the mill owner but an athlete of above average ability and sometime secretary of the Haslingden Athletic Club, saw him running with the train, and was so impressed by his seemingly effortless athletic ability, that he arranged for Warburton to run in a local sports meeting.

He showed such promise that he was signed up by the Haslingden Athletic Club, and in their colors competed in cross-country races and track events at local sports meetings all over the north of England. These meetings were an important feature in the social life of working people, who were avid supporters of sport of any kind. Mostly meetings were held on rough grass tracks marked out in a field, and such was the rarity of custom-built cinder tracks that he did not race on one until much later in his career.

In the early days of his career, all the events he took part in were restricted to the north of the country. His first trip south was in 1873, when he was twenty-eight years of age, and had been selected for a team competing in a North v. South meet held at the Lillie Bridge track in London. He finished in a lowly position, perhaps overawed by the whole experience of a long train journey and staying away from home for the first time.

He was undoubtedly a late developer, because at the age of 28, most runners had passed their peak, but as time will show, he had only just started. He traveled south again in 1874 to take part in a four-mile race at the English Amateur Championships, where he had to be content with second place. In 1878 he had a number of wins over the Southern Area Champion, J. Gibbs, and over one of the greatest runners of all time, Walter George. As a result, Warburton was acknowledged as Amateur Champion of England. He was an imposing figure, five feet ten inches tall, with a figure kept lean by years of training and diet, with good lungs and heart, helped no doubt by being a non-smoker and teetotaller.

He was at the height of his athletic powers, and acknowledged by his peers as one of the finest runners in the country. He had the distinction of being one of the few provincial working-class runners to win an Amateur Athletic Club race, as they were almost exclusively the reserve of university men. Instead of praising him, one so-called "gentlemen of the press" described him as a "plebeian runner," a polite way of saying he was of the lower classes, vulgar and common—the curse of the English class system was alive and well.

During this period of success as an amateur athlete, he continued working as a warehouseman in the mills, from 6 AM to 5:30 PM, five and a half days a week, somehow finding time to train and compete at week-ends and public holidays. The cost of strip, running shoes, and travel could not be met from his meager wages alone, so he was forced to supplement his income by selling some of the many prizes he won, and as was the custom of the day, received payment at some meetings for taking part in races that were fixed to the advantage of the bookmakers. As he became better known to the public, he would receive appearance money and generous travelling expenses from promoters.

These practices had become commonplace both in athletics and cycling, as the public, having more leisure time due to statutory holidays being introduced by the 1871 Bank Holiday Act, took a greater interest in sport, and consequently promoters wanted the finest athletes to compete at their meets, and were willing to pay for the privilege. Bookmakers were banned from sports grounds by the authorities, because betting, they claimed, encouraged race fixing. However, they turned a blind eye to their presence, as the public wanted to bet on the races, and if unable to do so, attendances at meets would have fallen dramatically.

Choppy's life in Haslingden was not all work, training, and competing. He even found time for romance. Being tall, handsome, athletic, and loquacious, he was popular with the ladies. However, it was not until he was in his late twenties that he started seriously courting a girl from his home town named Mary

Ann Johnson. Friendship blossomed into love, and they were married in St. James Church in Haslingden in 1874.

He was now almost thirty years of age, employed as a mill warehouseman on a low wage, and living at home with his parents in the Wagon and Horses public house on Church Street, Haslingden, where his father was the landlord. He was without capital, and now had the responsibility of finding a home for his wife. He had first-hand experience of the license trade, so the problem was solved by becoming the licensee of the Fisherman's Arms on Birley Street in Blackburn, the pub providing both accommodation and income.

The new life worked well, despite having to work seven days a week, from early in the morning until late at night. He still found time to train, and he joined the Blackburn Athletic Club, which enabled him to compete in local events. In 1879 his wife gave birth to a son, James (Jimmy) Allen. He was delivered without complications, and both mother and child were healthy.

Choppy was delighted to have a son to carry on the family name. However, the addition to the family brought added responsibility, and a need to increase his income. He was now thirty-four, and realized that the only way to earn some real money was to turn professional while he was still capable of competing at a high level.

During his many years in the sport, Warburton had made contacts with many managers and promoters throughout the country, but although he was outgoing and popular, he was an individualist and something of a loner. He listened to advice, sought council from fellow athletes, but always thought he knew what was best for him. He had never felt the need for a trainer, being content to set his own training schedule and diet. Despite his thirty-four years, he was still a naive boy from the provinces, unaware of the confidence tricksters, sharks, and villains that inhabited the professional sporting world, always looking for someone to make money for them.

This naivety made him extremely vulnerable—just how vulnerable he was going to discover when he was persuaded that

America was the country where big money could be made from running. So on the 19th July 1880 Choppy, accompanied by a friend, embarked on the steamship Wyoming bound for New York. On arrival, they were met by his brother George, who had gone to America to work in the cotton trade and had arranged accommodation and races for him to compete in. Warburton had been advised that being unknown outside his own country, he should take a number of trophies with him to prove to promoters how good he was. That was his first mistake.

His second mistake was being unaware of the oppressive heat and humidity that prevailed during the summer in most of the United States. He had, after all, spent a lifetime in the cold, damp climate of northern England. He was unable to train, and was dogged by ill health, so it was not until the end of August that he was able to compete in his first race. During the trip he ran at all distances from two to forty miles, and took part in several long-distance events that were so popular with the

"CHOPPY" WARBURTON.

Right: Fig. 1.3. This drawing of Choppy Warburton appeared in a 1894 issue of *Cycling* magazine.

15

American public. Out of the twelve races he competed in, he won seven.

He had originally planned on being in the country for three months, but because of circumstances beyond his control, his departure was delayed until the following year. When getting his luggage together in the hotel prior to returning home, he found that the trunk containing his trophies was missing, together with the trophies. He was told by the concierge that they had been impounded by the court pending a claim against him for payment of outstanding debts. He refuted the claim, and when the case came to court, the judge found in his favor. It was a moral victory, but only added further to his financial burden, as hotel costs had to be met while waiting for the case to be heard. To add to his woes, his delayed departure meant that he was not home in time for the birth of his daughter Mary Ann, born on the 13th December. When he finally arrived home, his wife, although glad he was finally back, was less than happy to have been left alone to run the business and cope with the physical discomforts of pregnancy and childbirth without the support of her husband.

The trip to America had been mildly successful from an athletic viewpoint, but a disaster financially, as the income generated came nowhere near to covering the expense of travel, hotels, and race entry fees that totaled nearly two-thousand dollars. His third and biggest mistake was to become involved with shysters and betting men who were only too pleased to lend him money—provided he ran to instructions, thus ensuring they got a good return on their investment. The problem was, he did not always follow instructions, and often won when he should have lost.

Consequently he was in such trouble, that he feared physical assault, so when booking his return passage on the steamship Germanic, he used an assumed name, and much to his relief when the boat sailed from New York on the 12th August 1881, his departure went unnoticed. He returned home to a hero's welcome, but an American newspaper told a different story:

His career in this country was a continued succession of sells, tricks, defeats, disgraces, and frauds. He was crooked all the way through after his first race, and ran in the interests of a gang of bullies and blacklegs, who told him when to win and when to lose, as best suited their betting books. That he was persecuted, plundered, and punished we admit, but he couldn't expect any better from the crowd he trained with. The very worst and meanest of the local sporting world were his associates and partners. That they fleeced him is most certainly true, as that Choppy fleeced and sold everybody who had anything to do with him.

So what was the real truth of his American odyssey? We shall probably never know exactly what happened, but he certainly got involved with the wrong crowd. Whether he had learned lessons for the future we shall see.

One thing we can be certain of is that he returned home exhausted and broke. He took a year out of competition, and spent the time resting and building up his neglected business. Although he was now a veteran athlete, at thirty-seven years of age, he was still confident he could make good money from running, so in the autumn of 1883 he once again sailed to America to compete in a variety of races from three miles to twelve-hour go-as-you-please matches.

During this trip he appears to have had no connection with the crowd of villains he was involved with during his first trip to the States, and because there were no reports in the American newspapers of the races he took part in, it is possible that he competed under a pseudonym, a practice common at the time among sportsmen trying to avoid the sins of the past catching up with them.

This second trip was reasonably profitable, with none of the traumatic events that had marred the first. He returned home in April 1884 and was back in action in June, when he made an attempt on the thirty-mile record. He made a brave effort, but failed to get anywhere near the record time. The following year, Warburton was appointed manager and trainer of athletics at the

Stanley Park Running Grounds in Liverpool, so he left the Fisherman's Arms, which had been the family home for eleven years, to take up a new challenge.

It must be assumed that his stay at the Stanley Grounds was unsuccessful, because over the next two years he managed several un- named taverns, to finish up in 1887 as landlord of the Eagle and Child public house in Whitefield, Manchester. During this unsettled period, he carried on competing in events all over the country, but the culminating effort of running a business, training, and racing was having a detrimental effect on the health of a man now in his mid-forties, and he began to suffer heart problems.

His final event was a veteran's race organized by a Sir John Dugdale-Astley, known as the "Sporting Baron." It was a handicap race over ten-miles. The rules stipulated that competitors had to be over fifty years of age, with a handicap of fifty-yards for each year over fifty, with suitable monetary prizes. It took place on the 28th November 1892 at the Stamford Bridge track in London.

Warburton justified his position as pre-race favorite, started from scratch, and won with ease. However an objection was lodged by one of the other competitors that Warburton was forty-seven, not fifty years old as he had claimed. He produced a copy of Choppy's birth certificate to substantiate his claim, and Choppy was disqualified. It appears that his fellow competitor was aware that he could be economic with the truth when it suited him, and had come armed with evidence to challenge the date of his birth. It was an embarrassing situation, and an ignominious end to his running career.

Chapter 2.

Choppy, the Coach

WITH HIS ATHLETIC CAREER now over, Choppy was faced with the problem of how to provide for his family. He was no longer a publican, and was living with his family at 198 Bolton Road, Salford, near Manchester. The census for 1891 lists the address as a shop which he seemed to have rented out, while the family occupied the rest of the premises. The rent from the shop provided a small income, but not enough to support his family, so he decided to set himself up as a trainer.

Right: Fig. 2.1. Choppy in Paris. An imposing figure, with a taste for flashy outfits and long overcoats.

During his running career it was the custom of promoters to combine athletics and cycle racing at the same event, and because he was successful, the competitors from both disciplines would seek his advice on training and diet. Consequently he had many contacts among runners and cyclists.

From his extensive experience as a long-distance runner he had learned that the disciplines of running and cycling required similar preparation, both physical and mental. Within the compass of knowledge available at the time, he was an advocate of specific training schedules to build up endurance and stamina, and appreciated the importance of recovery. He was a hard taskmaster and disciplinarian, expecting total obedience from his charges. He became a Svengali figure, seemingly exerting almost magical powers over his athletes.

In the beginning things were hard, and he took on anyone who was willing to pay for his advice—runners, cyclists, rowers, boxers, swimmers, and skaters. He even trained greyhounds for the Waterloo Cup, which had been held in Lancashire for many years. He was undoubtedly very competent in the physical conditioning of his charges and was able to instil that most elusive of emotions, confidence and self-belief. He was an extrovert and show-man, oozing self-confidence, and despite his lack of formal education, could express himself clearly and succinctly.

His first famous client was the cyclist F. J. ("Freddy") Osmond, the NCU champion from 1887 to 1891. Osmond had begun his racing career on a high-wheel, or ordinary, bicycle, and had successfully changed over to the safety bicycle when it became available. However, by 1892, when Warburton came to supervise his training, he was having trouble maintaining his form. They had training sessions on the tracks at Water-Orton, near Birmingham, and at Herne Hill in London, where later that year Osmond broke several professional records.

For a short period in the late 1890s, cycle racing behind pacers reigned supreme in the field of public entertainment. In velodromes all over Europe and America, thousands of people paid to watch the multi-manned pacing machines thundering around banked tracks, pulling the furiously pedaling racers behind them in a blaze of color and motion. They were the fastest men on earth; nothing, not even a racehorse, could reach such speeds. It was an exciting and dangerous spectacle. None of the riders wore helmets or protective clothing, and with as many as six teams on the track at the same time, crashes were frequent and spectacular, often resulting in serious, and sometimes fatal, injuries.

The racers became highly paid stars, sharing the same billing as enjoyed by music-hall artistes, with hordes of fans following every moment of their lives through the sporting and national press, whether it was a sporting achievement, romance, or marriage breakup. Young riders reading of these exploits were inspired to follow in the footsteps of these stars in an attempt to escape a life of drudgery and deprivation. They found that if they had proven athletic talent, the quickest way to success was to sign up with an experienced trainer/manager.

By 1893, it had become apparent that Paris was rapidly becoming the center of international professional bicycle racing, both on the road and on the track. Consequently, Choppy moved his operations to Paris, where he established working

Right: Fig. 2.2. F. J. "Freddy" Osmond, who had been NCU champion from 1887 until 1891, became Choppy Warburton's first famous client.

relationships with track operators and manufacturers.

In that same year, a young amateur rider named Arthur Linton, aged 23, from a small Welsh mining town, made his first appearance in London riding in the 24 hour Cuca Cup. Although he displayed a raw talent, and put up a sterling performance against the seasoned opponents, Linton was aware he needed expert coaching. Hearing that Choppy Warburton was the best in the business, he decided that this was the man he needed to become his mentor. So, armed with his new professional licence, he made his way to Paris to persuade Warburton to sign him up, which he duly did, giving him the nickname "The Collier Boy."

Keen to get the raw youngster some publicity, and as ever the consummate showman, Warburton looked for a spectacular event to bring his man to public attention. He knew that William Cody, known as Buffalo Bill, was in town with his spectacular Wild West Show and was keen to incorporate the fashionable bicycle into his performances. He had already put his top star, Annie Oakley, on a bicycle, shooting at targets while she pedalled around the ring, and his wife had ridden a horse against a team of women cyclists, with the girls winning every time.

Probably the most spectacular was a match with Cody riding against the French tandem pair of Fournier and Gaby for a purse of 20,000 francs. Warburton arranged a meeting with Cody and persuaded the American to stage an event where he would ride against Linton. The cycling extravaganzas were all staged on the horse track at the Vélodrome de la Seine in front of huge audiences. The results of the races were immaterial, as they were all "arranged," but the public were treated to some exciting theater, Arthur Linton got some publicity, Warburton made some money, and everyone was happy.

Arthur was delighted with his Parisian debut, and was later joined in the city by his brothers Tom and Sam, who also became part of the Warburton menage. Both boys had been members of the Aberaman Cycling Club, as had another of their colleagues, Jimmy Michael, who had made a sensational debut at the age of eighteen by beating all the top riders in the Surrey 100 at Herne Hill on the 30th June 1894, and in the process set a new record for the distance.

Although Jimmy's next two appearances on the track were disappointing, Warburton sensed his potential, and invited him to join his ever-expanding group of riders in Paris. Jimmy Michael was just over five foot tall and weighed in at seven stone ten pounds (94 lbs.), but a lot of power was packed into that small package, and with an eye to the publicity potential of

Top left and above: Figs. 2.3 and 2.4. Buffalo Bill's son, William Cody Jr., competes against high-wheel rider Josef Fischer, 1893.

Left: Fig. 2.5. Annie Oakley poster, showing her shooting her rifle from a bicycle (top right detail).

marketing a vertically challenged rider, Warburton gave him the title "The Mighty Midget."

They all signed contracts for the French Gladiator Cycle Company and lived in accommodations provided by the company in Paris, close to the factory and the two main cycle racing tracks. The establishment was run like a hotel, with food and laundry services provided. To ensure they were not tempted by the fleshpots of the city, their lives were strictly monitored.

By this time, Warburton, a devoted family man, had found accommodation for his wife and two children in the city, as he missed them terribly when they lived in England. At the weekends, he would take his son Jimmy to the tracks, where he was fascinated by the color and dash of cycle racing—he later took up the sport, and eventually became a professional rider, trained and managed by his father.

With such a group of talented riders under his care, Warburton drew up a training schedule and dietary regime for each of them. Without exception all the performances of the riders under his tutelage improved, some becoming national and world champions. So what was his formula for success?

Ever since the early days of his athletic career, Warburton had been secretive about his training methods and the contents of the little black bottle he always carried. By the time he had become a full-time professional trainer and manager, he had succeeded in developing these secretive traits to such an extent that many of his methods were considered magical. He was aware of the impression he made, and went to great lengths to maintain it. He loved to draw attention to himself by wild, extravagant gestures, and his language was colorful and expressive. He spoke colloquial French with a strong Lancashire accent, much to the delight of his Gallic audience. Despite his flamboyance, he was devoted and fiercely loyal to his riders, and would defend them from any criticism.

When he came to live in Paris, he adopted the Parisian way of life, grew a fashionable walrus moustache, dressed in the latest style, with a taste for flashy waistcoats and long overcoats.

He was, to use the Victorian expression, "a bit of a card."

Throughout his career, he had kept a cuttings book and copious notes on people, places, details of training schedules, training etc. He told how one day he would write a book that would astonish people in the sporting world. Unfortunately the book was never written and the collection of cuttings disappeared after his death, so we will never know what, if any, revelations he would have disclosed.

Fortunately some idea of his views on training and an outline of the role of the various types of trainer and manager, were disclosed during an interview he gave to a reporter of the monthly magazine *The Hub* in October 1897. In the introduction

Right: Fig. 2.6. German caricature warning of the dangers of motor-paced cycle racing, which was all the rage in the 1890s.

Left: Fig. 2.7. The dangers of motor-paced racing were evidenced by this horrific 1909 accident in Berlin, in which nine people were killed and 52 injured.

25

to the interview the reporter is reluctant to give the identity of the interviewee, but the description of the man leaves no doubt that the subject was Choppy Warburton. The article begins with a physical description of the trainer, and then continues in the form of an interview:

Of course, you know, there are two or three kinds of trainer, and what one class will do another can't or won't. There is, first of all, what you might almost call the amateur trainer—the individual who hangs about dressing rooms in his spare time and rubs down whosoever shouts for him, receiving a sixpence or so for his trouble. He is anybody's man, and does just as he is told, and—well, yes, as you say, he is quite harmless.

The next class includes the men who have charge of separate riders, who are engaged by them, and who do nothing else but look after their masters, rub them down before they go on the track and afterward, see to their things, regulate their hours of work and diet, and so on. These are experienced fellows who know what they are doing and are paid for what they do, and the more prizes the rider wins the better they are paid.

The third class [to which Warburton belonged] is a small one and rather a good job too. The trainers who comprise it are old stagers who have forgotten more about the game than most of the others will ever learn. They know the ins and outs of everything, good and bad and make full use of their knowledge. You don't find these men engaged at so much a week. Instead of that it often happens that they engage the riders themselves at so much a week and take all the profits. I have a splendid instance of this in my mind at the present time, which I will not, however, repeat, though I am speaking now entirely from fact.

These men go about with their eyes very wide open: and when they see a well-made lad, sound in wind and limb, who sits on his machine as if he were part of it, they take stock of him, and sometimes, if they think he is good enough, they take him in hand. He is simply so much raw material at the commencement and possibly could not win a handicap race from the limit mark, but two or three months under his trainer may make a veritable champion of him. He [the trainer] sets himself at the very outset to study the lad's anatomy, till at length he knows exactly what he is dealing with, and knows every weak place and every strong one. It is no exaggeration to say, that a trainer such as I have described can find out more about his pupil in this way in a month that a doctor could ever do. Then he proceeds to build up the weak places and make them strong like the others, till at length his subject is muscularly perfect.

He puts him on a special diet and gets his stomach into good working order, and nobody but a rider and trainer knows what a wonderful extent a perfect stomach contributes to success, and how difficult it is to get into really first-class working order and keep it like that. Next the wind is attended to, till by-and-by the lad is as fine in wind and limb as he can be. Regular hours, regular work, and sprints on the track, good food, and a little attention to other exercises, such as the skipping rope, boxing, and so on, and speed quickly comes if the man is good for anything at all. It is moonshine about racing men being born and not made. If taken in hand soon enough, and treated in this way by a man who knows what he is doing, they can be turned out by the dozen. It is useless for the riders to try to do it themselves as some do. One of the very finest riders at middle distance, in either England or France at the present time, was made to order only a few months ago by a trainer in this way.

Oh yes, the trainers are complete masters of such men, in the early weeks of their success at any rate, and there can be no doubt but that the masters annex the greater portion of the prize-money. They are like owners of race horses. There was a public complaint, you know, by a prominent rider some time ago, that his trainer had got a lot of his prize-money and would not give it to him. With men so much under their trainers' control it cannot be at all surprising that races are not always ridden on the riders' merits. If anybody for any reason does not want one of the cracks to win, the individual he sees about the matter is his "boss," and it is made all right. Sometimes however the race is of such importance, that even the trainer dare not approach his man and with a view to squaring it; so then he may resort to methods of preventing his victory without his knowing it.

When a rider has been brought out by an old hand in this way and has made him into a crack; that is when the trouble begins between the two. It is the money question. The pupil is inclined to kick over the traces. However by this time each is completely at the other's mercy; the trainer knowing enough about the man to make it very uncomfortable for him if a quarrel took place. Gradually the system of dividing the gains is changed and the trainer looks out for fresh blood to work with. You may have heard now and again about So-and-so having a string of young riders under him. He is searching for his next flier.

When Warburton first took his riders to race in France, he found:

They [the French] do not train very hard, but when in a race try every time. My lads Arthur Linton and Jimmy Michael have been a lesson to them, up early in the morning, and after a mutton chop and a couple of eggs they do their work... with never failing regularity. My men win, and it is said that I give them some mysterious drinks, they wonder what my drink is of course, when a man is riding a machine, hour after hour, he requires something nourishing. My old running days have taught me something, I have a food of my own, which is both meat and drink, and which is warm, I never give the stomach anything cold at such a time.

Knowing of Warburton's secretive manner, can these disclosures be believed? By the time of the interview, all the other trainers had witnessed his training methods and indeed were copying them, so it has to be accepted that these were his methods. The only secret left was the contents of his little black bottle. It was a secret that was eventually to contribute to his downfall, and blight his place in sporting history.

In the article he freely admits that "races are not always ridden on the riders' merits..." In other words, it was not uncommon to fix a race; this was how it worked. A group of riders would get together to arrange the result of a race, use a third party to spread the betting among the bookmakers, make a killing, and share the spoils. It is possible that Warburton was that third party and took his share of the ill-gotten gains. Strangely, he makes no mention of the fourth class of manager that was prevalent at that time, who looked after what was known as "maker's amateurs."

The system was well organized: A bicycle manufacturer would appoint a manager whose job it was to seek out successful amateur racers to ride their machines. The manager was often a sporting journalist, who could openly attend race meetings, ostensibly to report on the event, check on his charges, and look out for any promising riders to add to his stable, without arousing the suspicions of the authorities. The manager was paid a handsome salary, plus commission based on the success

Above: Fig. 2.8. While other trainers, like this one, were seen on bicycles themselves, not so Choppy, who never learned to ride a bicycle himself.

Left: Fig. 2.9. Jimmy Michael, held up by a young Choppy look-alike.

of his riders. The amount the rider received depended on his ability to make a good bargain with the manager.

Some riders made separate arrangements with makers of frames, tires, chains, and other bicycle equipment. The manager would pay his riders the agreed principal sum monthly in cash, with commission payments made at the end of the season, but not before the rider had presented full details of race results, records broken, and names of opponents. Some top riders could make more than £1,000 a year, plus prize money, cups, and trophies. Riders were allowed to keep the bicycles and equipment supplied to them, so at the end of the season, track changing rooms across the country became cycle jumble sales crowded with clubmen looking for a bargain.

The manufacturers of course vehemently denied any involvement in this sham amateurism, despite loudly acclaiming the achievements of certain riders shown to be using their products in advertising. There is no evidence to suggest that during their early years of racing, Jimmy Michael and the Linton brothers were ever maker's amateurs, but born into such a financially deprived section of society, it would be surprising if they did not grab any opportunity to improve their monetary situation, as did many of their colleagues. Some riders were inevitably caught transgressing the rules by the authorities: Early in 1894 "Jack" Stocks was charged by the NCU of "being affiliated with the bicycle trade," and his license was withdrawn. Bans did not prevent riders from competing and earning a living. A rider could simply take out a professional license and continue riding for the same bicycle maker he had been riding for previously.

One subject Warburton omitted was how many training miles his riders were expected to do, both on the road and on the track. Since all their racing was paced, they must have trained behind pacers at racing speed. There is no mention either of the bicycles they rode, positioning, or gearing. We know that Warburton had never learned to ride a bicycle himself, and his lack of knowledge of anything mechanical was legendary. Presumably someone in the Gladiator factory must have assumed responsibility for setting up and maintaining the bicycles for individual riders. This inability was highlighted in a report in *The Cyclist* on the 29th December of an incident during a meet organized by the Syndicate of Speedmen in Paris:

> Strange for a man who became so famous in the world of cycle sport that he scarcely knew how to mount a bicycle. He offered to mount a tandem behind the French ace Albert Champion and take part in a two kilometre race. Much to the amusement of the crowd he scrambled onto the machine, clung on to Champion and in this manner wobbled to the finish, coming last as expected.

At that time, in the constant search for speed, the majority of middle- and long-distance track races were paced by teams of tandems, triplets, quadruplets, and quintuplets. To give the competitors every advantage, the pacers had to be in top physical condition. Many were top-class riders who had nearly reached the end of their careers and found that by joining a pacing team they could earn more pacing than they could if they continued racing. The Gladiator Cycle Company employed excellent pacing teams, all trained by Warburton. However, as motive engineering developed, manual pacing was gradually replaced by tandems fitted with electric motors and petrol engines to supplement the pedaling effort, and consequently speeds increased. Traditionally competitors used standard track machines with a higher gear ratio for paced racing, and it was not until the British rider Albert "Jenny" Walters joined Gladiator that a special "stayer" bicycle was created.

The year 1895 was the pinnacle of Warburton's success as a trainer/manager. Jimmy Michael, his star rider, rode twenty-eight races with twenty-two wins, including a victory over Constant Huret, the French champion, in a 100 mile race in Paris, and when appearing at the Catford track in London, he broke the two and three-mile records together with the six-hour race, during which he broke all English records up to 144 miles. In August of that year, during a racing trip to Cologne, Germany,

Michael won the 100 km event to become World Middle-Distance Cycling Champion.

His confidence and rebelliousness grew along with his success, and Warburton found him more and more difficult to handle. His failure to turn up at scheduled race meetings was reported by the promoters to the authorities, who threatened Warburton with heavy financial penalties should Michael continue to absent himself from meets without prior notification.

It was not such a successful year for Arthur Linton, as he suffered a knee injury, had a disagreement with Warburton over money, which caused a rift between them, but through negotiations by a third party they came to an amicable agreement that allowed their partnership to continue. Tom Linton enjoyed a successful, if not spectacular year, with many good wins in both England and mainland Europe.

Warburton was made welcome in every track in Europe. When he strolled into the *pelouse*, or track-center, his appearance was greeted with thunderous applause and enthusiastic acclaim. He loved the attention of a crowd; he sought it and reveled in it. On one occasion he calmed the fury of disappointed spectators, and probably saved the Buffalo Vélodrome from destruction, by climbing onto a chair and haranguing the rebellious crowd in a mixture of French and Lancastrian English, accompanied by extravagant gestures. No one understood what he was saying—they did not need to: he entertained them, and they laughed and were pacified.

Stella Bloch, a German sports journalist who knew him well, reported in *Cycling* in 1926:

> He was a fearless fighting cock, and brooked no interference; he was always in the wars. Once he so infuriated the French racing men that they built a figure to resemble him, stuffed it and surrounded it with flammable matter, carried it in solemn procession all around the velodrome, and just as solemnly set fire to it, and burnt Choppy in effigy, watching him crumble away with glee.

The ever-expanding team of riders created an expanding quantity of paperwork. There were contracts to draft, travel arrangements to be made, hotels to book, pacers located and engaged, and a million other administrative tasks that required attention. As telephones were not yet available, contact with promoters, sponsors, and riders had to be by letter, and to handle the voluminous correspondence in English, French, German, Italian, and Russian, Warburton engaged a charming multilingual secretary of Russian origin who was faultless in the execution of her duties. Much to the amusement of his colleagues, when the office closed, the lady was later discovered performing erotic dances in the Trianion Music Hall in Paris, under the stage name of Mademoiselle Wanda.

1896 was a year of triumph, disaster, and sorrow for both Warburton and his star riders. Jimmy Michael rode successfully with wins in England, France, and Germany, but his relationship with his manager was under strain. When he first joined Warburton, he was very young and inexperienced in money matters. He was flattered to be taken under the wing of the man who was considered the best trainer in the world. The terms of his contract were simple: Warburton would undertake to train him to

Below: Fig. 2.10. J. W. Stocks at the Crystal Palace track with the Dunlop pacing team in 1897.

championship level, he would be paid a good monthly salary, plus bonuses for winning important races. All travel costs and hotel bills would be paid by his manager, with pacers, bicycles and equipment provided by a sponsor. All Michael had to do was train to a schedule, ride his bike to orders, and do as he was told.

At the beginning this was an attractive proposition for a boy from a mining village in Wales—money to spend, wined and dined in the top restaurants, staying in the best hotels, and receiving the adoration of fans whenever he appeared in the street or on the track. It is impossible to know exactly what salary he received, but when talking to competitors in the changing rooms, Michael became aware that his salary was small compared to the income Warburton derived from riders' fees, and payments from promoters and sponsors, which enabled him to enjoy the lifestyle of a major celebrity. Michael tried to negotiate better terms with Warburton, but without success, so he began to explore what other options were open to him should he be able to break his contract.

During the early part of the year, Arthur Linton competed in a number of track races culminating in a six-day race at the Agricultural Hall in London, when he covered 419 miles to take victory. Warburton no doubt thought the mileage covered at racing speeds would be ideal preparation for Linton's first major race of the year, the inaugural Paris–Roubaix, held in April. Linton rode well, and despite several falls managed to finish in fourth place, ahead of some of the best roadmen in Europe. It was his first major road race, and he impressed the journalists, and worried the opposition, by his determined and courageous riding over some of the worst roads in France. When he lined up at the start of the fearsome 369 mile long Bordeaux–Paris in May, he was full of confidence and secure in the knowledge of his ability to win. The bookmakers decided that the German Josef Fischer and the Frenchman Gaston Rivierre were favorites, but a lot of money went on Linton too.

The pace was fast and furious from the gun, with Fischer and Rivierre sharing the lead, but as they passed the 100 mile mark, the German hit a dog and was unable to continue. Rivierre had by this time fallen back, so Linton was now in the lead and rode on alone. By the time he reached the feeding station at Orleans, where Warburton was waiting, he was in considerable distress. Alarmed at the condition his rider was in, Warburton cried out, "It is all over now," and thought he was finished. He nevertheless cleaned him down, gave him something to drink, and at Linton's insistence, sent him on his way. Seemingly revived, he continued to Paris to win the race in 21 hours 18 seconds. An objection was lodged by Rivierre that Linton had not kept to the official course. The objection was upheld, and they were declared joint winners.

Because the Bordeaux–Paris race was considered the Blue Riband of professional cycling, it confirmed Linton's claim to the title of "Champion Cyclist of the World." All the cycling journals, including *Cycling* and the *Scottish Cyclist*, gave reports of the race and praised the courage of Linton for continuing the race after his collapse at Orleans; there was no hint of impropriety. However, some time after the event, rumor began to circulate that Warburton had given Linton a stimulant from his little black bottle at the feeding station. In the 28th July issue of *Cyclers News*, a writer styling himself as "One who knows" reported:

I saw him at Tours, halfway through the race, at midnight, where he came in with glassy eyes and tottering limbs, and in a high state of nervous excitement. I then heard him swear, a very rare occurrence with him, but after a rest he was off again, though none of us expected he would go very far. At Orleans at five o'clock in the morning, Choppy and I looked after a wreck, a corpse as Choppy called him, yet he had sufficient energy, heart, pluck, call it what you will, to enable him to gain 18 minutes on the last four and a half miles of hilly road.

Neither the sport's controlling authorities nor the race organizer, *Le Vélo*, made any comment, or indeed took any action against Linton or Warburton as a result of the allegations. It must be remembered that at that time athletes were free to administer whatever substance they wanted. The authorities were aware that riders took drugs, but never saw fit to issue a list of proscribed substances. All the people close to him believed that Warburton's little black bottle contained only water, or at the worst one of his herbal mixtures. If indeed Linton had taken trimethyl, as has been suggested, it is feasible, but highly unlikely, that he administered the stimulant himself, without Warburton's knowledge; it is impossible to know. Although winning the race was at first a triumph for Linton and Warburton, it eventually turned into a tragedy for them both.

Linton stayed in France after Bordeaux–Paris, and during a race in Paris in June he broke the 50 and 100 km national track records. Despite Warburton's pleas that he should rest, he returned to London in July to compete in the Catford three-day "Gold Vase" race, during which he collapsed, complaining of sickness, and was unable to finish. There is no doubt that he was exhausted and completely drained after Bordeaux–Paris, and should have listened to his trainer's advice and taken a complete rest.

Warburton was aware of the importance of including rest and recuperation periods into the training schedules of his riders. During his athletic career, he discovered that he was incapable of repeatedly running long distances without periods of complete rest, so insisted his riders follow his example. Although the disciplines of running and cycling are similar, they require totally different approaches in preparation, so regretfully the cyclists in his care suffered from his lack of knowledge and understanding of the sport. This was not wilful neglect and something peculiar to Warburton, who, for his time, was very advanced in his theories on training. However, athletes would have to wait another generation before scientific training methods were developed.

The second major event of the year for Warburton's men, after Bordeaux–Paris, were the Chain Races at the Catford track in London, where they competed with moderate success. However, the long-term ramifications that emanated from both races proved to be disastrous. Before examining the Chain Races in detail, it is interesting to look at the reasons for staging the races, and the people involved in their promotion and organization.

William Spears Simpson had invented a bicycle drive-chain that he claimed would revolutionize the sport and pastime of cycling, and decided to organize an event in London that would promote his invention. In his search for a suitable venue, he made contact with the owner of a cycle racing track in the north of the capital. The owner was well known to Warburton, as they had negotiated terms for his riders to appear at his track on numerous occasions. At that time there were several tracks in the capital, although few were built upon the initiative of one man. The cycle racing track in north London and the story of its conception and construction is a good example of the entrepreneurial skills of a Victorian businessman who became involved in the sport to enhance his business.

Right: Fig. 2.11. Drawing published in Le Cycle of 5 January 1896, showing "Choppy's last instructions to his charge [Jimmy Michael]."

Derniers conseils de Choppy à son poulain.

The Wood Green track in north London was the brainchild of Albert Walter Gamage, a shrewd businessman, founder and owner of the monumental department store in Holborn known as Gamages. The business had been built on profits made by selling bicycles, accessories, cycling and sports clothing, and any other merchandise purchased by hard negotiation and offered at bargain prices. To further promote his cycling and sports empire, he became a member of several cycling and athletic clubs, including the Finsbury Cycling Club and the Polytechnic Cycling and Athletic Club, both based in London. He was an active cyclist, generous supporter of cycling and athletics, and donor of many trophies and awards that bore his name. In an official capacity, he served as a judge for the National Cyclists Union (NCU) at racing events, so he was well known to the people who controlled the sport.

In 1894 he decided to build his own sports stadium, and after an intensive search for a suitable site purchased Nightingale Hall, which stood in extensive grounds off Bounds Green Lane, Wood Green. The hall had stood empty for some years; it was derelict and beyond repair, so it was demolished to make way for a cycle racing and athletic track built to the design of H. J. Swindley, a journalist for *The Cyclist* magazine, and built by J. O. McQuone of Scarborough. Financing the building at a costs of over £18,000 was a massive undertaking for Gamage, but his judgement in business had been sound from his humble beginnings, so he was willing to take the risk. The concrete cycle track was 3.5 laps to the mile, with 120-yard straights and 8 foot banking, making it one of the fastest tracks in the country. The covered grandstand seating 1,500 spectators was situated on the south-east home straight, and there was a smaller uncovered stand for 300 on the opposite side. The whole stadium could accommodate 10,000 spectators. There was a restaurant, a licensed bar, a café with outside seating, a bandstand, and areas for traders to set up stalls.

The Gamage Cycling and Athletic Club was provided with a fine clubhouse under the grandstand, complete with billiard room. Work commenced on site early in 1895 and was scheduled to be completed by the Bank Holiday in June the same year. The track was well served by public transport: by omnibus along Bounds Green Lane and by trains of the Great Eastern Railway to Alexandra Palace Station and of the Great Northern Railway to Wood Green Station. The track augmented the racecourse and other sporting amenities at Alexandra Palace, making north London the Mecca for sporting events in the capital.

An operating company was formed, called The North London Cycling and Athletic Grounds Ltd., with the controlling number of shares held by Gamage. The opening ceremony was performed by Gamage on Whit Monday, 7th June 1895 in front of a capacity crowd, who had come to watch a full day of entertainment of cycle racing, athletics, and novelty events.

The sport and pastime of cycling was very popular, but racing on the public highway was seen by the NCU as a working-class activity, and liable to frighten old ladies and horses. So in December 1887 the NCU had passed a motion which expressed "disapproval of the growing practice of racing on public roads." As a result of this stricture, promoters turned their attention to track racing, and thus created a popular spectator sport with a massive following. Gamage proved to be an imaginative and innovative promoter. Events were held every week during the summer months, and the London cycling and athletic clubs were encouraged to use the track for training and their own championships.

Because of the success of the industrial revolution and the expansion of the Empire, the British working man was given more freedom and money to spend on leisure activities, and Bank Holidays were seen as a time for pleasure and enjoyment. Gamage saw these holidays as an opportunity to make money, and organized spectacular events at the Wood Green track with that purpose in mind.

For the 1896 Easter holiday, he organized a series of meetings under the auspices of the Gamage Cycling and Athletic Club. Among the top professional riders engaged were three of

Warburton's men: Tom Linton, Albert "Jenny" Walters, and Arthur Chase, riding their sponsor's Gladiator bicycles fitted with Simpson Lever Chains, as were their opponents, "Jack" Platt-Betts and Charley Barden. The Friday meeting was a low-key event, although 53 entrants were down to ride, and according to the local newspaper, the *Wood Green Herald*, the racing was watched by some 12,000 people. Although the riders gave a spirited performance, and broke several national records, it was obvious they were holding back for the major event planned for Monday.

On the Monday, the riders appeared again in a medley of races, but the much advertised big event of the week-end was the 20-mile scratch race between Tom Linton and "Jack" Platt-Betts. Both riders were paced by quads and triplets. Linton took the lead in the early laps, but at three miles Platt-Betts caught and passed him. Linton, finding his pacers too slow, left them behind and went off in hot pursuit. His brave attempt failed, and by the time he had rejoined his pacers, Platt-Betts was thirty yards ahead. Despite many spirited attempts, and loud encouragement from the spectators, Linton was unable to get on terms with his opponent, leaving Platt-Betts to cross the finishing line some half a lap ahead, with a winning time of 41 minutes 56 seconds. The race was described by the reporter of *Cycling* magazine as "the keenest struggle we've ever seen."

Gamage had seen how successful women's racing had been at the Olympia indoor track during the early part of the year, so he engaged the whole troupe to compete in the first ever outdoor race for women in England. The female riders liked riding at Wood Green, because Gamage treated them as serious athletes, and paid generous start and prize money. The ladies from Britain put up a spirited performance against their rivals from France. The event was much appreciated by the spectators, who cheered and applauded every race.

Always the innovator, Gamage organized what he called the "Daisy Races," with mixed pairs of men and women mounted on tandems. This was an inspired piece of promotion, because the song "Daisy Bell" was a huge hit at the time, due to it being adopted by the Music Hall star Miss Katie Lawrence. As the riders circled the track, the Wood Green Military Town Band accompanied the riders with a lively rendition of the song, and was soon joined by the singing voices of the crowd and riders, turning the event into a riot of noise and color.

Women's and mixed-sex races were forbidden under NCU rules, as indeed was trackside betting, but as Gamage was one of their officials, and a wealthy and influential businessman, a blind-eye was turned to the benefit of all.

For the Whitsun Bank Holiday, he organized a series of races that became known as the "Gamage Professional Tournaments." It was a spectacular event with 25 male and 13 female riders. There were also athletic events and cyclists against runners competitions. Food and drink was available, and the spectators were entertained, as usual, by the Wood Green Military Town Band. These big promotions were very popular, the stands and enclosures filled to capacity, spectators giving verbal support for the riders, the cries of vendors, bookmakers shouting the odds, and the band blasting out the latest tunes.

The nearby Nightingale Hotel was used regularly by Gamage to entertain important guests, promoters, officials, and riders, together with their managers after the events. The leading riders enjoyed the same following as film stars and top sports people do today, and they expected to be wined and dined by promoters. There is no doubt that many a deal was agreed and contracts signed over brandy at the Nightingale.

William Spears Simpson was a wealthy eccentric inventor. In appearance he was an imposing figure, tall, stout and bearded, with hair worn down to his collar and a taste for wide-brimmed hats and long-tailed coats. Early in 1895 he had caused a sensation in the world of cycling by proclaiming that he had invented a drive-chain that would make a rider go faster with less effort, a device that became known as the Simpson Lever Chain. So confident was he of success, that a factory was set up in Draycott,

Derbyshire, with plush offices at 119, Regent Street in the heart of London's West End.

Although Simpson was a wealthy man in his own right, he had no intention of risking his own money on the venture, and managed to secure financial backing from the charismatic corporate fraudster Ernest Terah Hooly. This enabled him to launch a huge advertising campaign, planned to culminate in a spectacular event where a team of riders mounted on bicycles fitted with lever chains would compete against a team on machines fitted with standard roller chains. Simpson wanted the event to be held in London, the centre of track racing in the world at that time.

He was so confident of success that he published a challenge in the national and sporting press that he would wager £1,000 against £100 that riders of his chain would win four out of six races, over distances from 1 to 100 miles. In addition, if no accident occurred to the Simpson riders, he would lay a further £1,000 that they would win all the races and beat the world record in every race (weather permitting). This declaration was

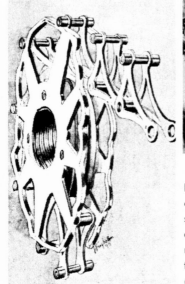

Left and above: Figs. 2.12 and 2.13. Details of the Simpson Lever Chain and its special sprocket on the rear wheel, which, though claimed to increase the rider's speed, did nothing of the sort (left), and an overview of the chain and chainring combination (above).

just another example of Simpson's flamboyant outbursts, and not to be taken seriously. The main challenge, however, was over three events—five miles, one hour, and fifty miles, and was advertised as such.

Gamage heard of Simpson's intentions and wanted the event for his Wood Green track, so on the 6th November 1895 they met in London to negotiate terms and the type of races the competitors would contest. At the outset of the meeting, Simpson declared that he favored the track at Catford, in South East London, which had opened in May that year, because with its size of three laps to a mile and sweeping banked ends, it would be better suited to accommodate the long wheelbase, multi-manned machines that were to be used to pace the riders.

Simpson also wanted the racing to be in the form of time-trials against the clock, but Gamage strongly objected, stating that the public would expect match-racing, man-against-man contests. Despite vigorous negotiations, Simpson got his way over the venue, but conceded that match racing would provide a more exciting public spectacle. It was agreed that Gamage would supply the racing strip for both teams of riders and pacers

Right: Fig. 2.14.
Toulouse-Lautrec
sketch showing
William Spears
Simpson (right) with
Jimmy Michael.

from his store in Holborn, so he too would get something out of the event.

Simpson then successfully negotiated with the Catford Cycling Club for use of their track, and waited impatiently for the challenge to be accepted. He did not have long to wait: early in 1896 he was approached by Dr. F. F. MacCabe, a well-known Dublin sportsman and publisher of the magazine *Irish Field*. MacCabe was an experienced racing cyclist who had come to England in 1890 with an Irish team, referred to as the "Irish Brigade," that rode machines fitted with the new pneumatic tires. The Irish Brigade had done much to popularize the acceptance of the pneumatic tires. Simpson accepted the challenge, and agreed that the contest would be held under NCU rules. A date was fixed for Saturday 6th June 1896, and the contest was given the grandiose title of the "Simpson Lever Chain Challenge," soon to be known to all cycling race enthusiasts as the "Chain Races." He engaged John Dring, an experienced cycle-race entrepreneur, to organize the event.

After signing the contract, Simpson went to Paris to meet his French agent Louis Bougle at the offices of his company at 25 Boulevard Haussmann. Bougle was a colorful character, who as well as being an astute businessman, was something of an art lover and an Anglophile. He dressed in the English manner and had adopted the name L. B. Spoke because it suggested a connection with bicycles and sounded vaguely English.

Together, they visited the Gladiator bicycle factory in the Rue Brunel, who were making frames specially adapted to take the lever chain. Gladiator had under contract some of the best riders and pacers in the world-Welshmen Jimmy Michael, Arthur and Tom Linton, Englishmen "Jack" Platt-Betts and "Jenny" Walters, and Frenchmen Albert Champion, Constant Huret, and Gaston Rivierre.

The riders and pacers were all under the care of Warburton, who was paid to keep them in top physical condition. When in Paris, they all lodged in the company hostel in the Avenue Philippe near the Gladiator factory. It was decided that the

Simpson Lever Ch
Jimmy Michael,
Robert Protin, th
be made on the
team of some si
lets, and a quint
the same strip—
and shorts.

The Welsh ri
their chests, pr
whole team, c
equipment, left
ling by train an

The Little Blac

chain. Simpson engaged hir
mother in May 1896, Toulo

I have two or three
there (London) f
bicyclists who
channel. I
make a
desti

The machines were conveyed to the
delivery van and the team by train to Catford railway station,
allowing them time to get acquainted with the track and settled
in their hotel.

Travelling with the team was the diminutive French graphic
artist Henri Toulouse-Lautrec, accompanied by his friend Tristan
Bernard. He had been introduced to Simpson by Louis Bougle,
who, having seen the artists' poster work plastered all over Paris,
thought he could create a sensational poster advertising the

Right: Fig. 2.15.
Toulouse-Lautrec's
original sketch for
the Simpson Lever
Chain poster,
showing
Zimmerman and
Choppy
Warbuton (left),
Jimmy Michael
(on the bike), and
Frantz Reichel
observing.

immediately. In a letter to his
use-Lautrec wrote:

> big deals with bicycle companies. I stayed
> om Thursday to Monday. I was with a team of
> ve gone to defend the flag on the other side of the
> pent three days outdoors and have come back here to
> poster advertising Simpson's Lever Chain, which may be
> ned to be a sensational success.

ulouse-Lautrec was by this time already a follower of the
sport. Many of his friends were cyclists who enjoyed not only
the bicycle as the latest fashion statement, but also as a new-
found expression of freedom. His friend Tristan Bernard, the
popular playwright, former amateur boxer, chief editor of the
Journal Des Vélocipèdistes, and director of the Vélodrome Buffalo in Neuilly, who later managed the Vélodrome de la Seine in
Levallois-Perrel, was the man who had introduced Toulouse-
Lautrec to cycle racing. Bernard said:

> Lautrec often came to the [cycle] races. He would meet me on
> Sunday; we would lunch together and go off to one of the stadi-
> ums. I would let him into the enclosure along with the officials,
> but he usually went off and sat on the lawn. I think the results
> interested him little, but he was fascinated by the setting and the
> people.

Toulouse-Lautrec did many sketches of the riders during practice and on the day of the race. He sketched Jimmy Michael several times; perhaps he felt an affinity with the rider as they were
both "vertically challenged." Fortunately, most of the sketches
have survived and are held in the Musée Toulouse-Lautrec in
Albi, his birthplace in southwest France. The design for the "La
Chaine Simpson" poster was worked out back in his studio in
Paris. The first attempt featured Jimmy Michael in the fore-
ground in typical pose, sitting almost upright on his machine

with trademark toothpick in mouth. Arthur Zimmerman and Choppy Warburton are on the left, with sports journalist Frantz Reichel, watch in hand, on the right. The layout was fine, but the content was not acceptable to Simpson and Bougle, because the bicycle was drawn incorrectly and, the biggest mistake of all, it included neither Simpson nor Bougle. Lautrec, however, was pleased with the result from an artistic viewpoint and had a limited edition of 200 printed at his own expense.

The final layout included all the elements required by the client. In the background can be seen the Catford Track, the band of the Honorary Artillery Company, the large dominating presence of W. S. Simpson, and the dapper figure of Louis Bougle. As we shall see shortly, Jimmy Michael failed ignominiously in his event, so the final composition featured Constant Huret as the central figure. The poster campaign was extraordinarily successful, but not in the way Simpson had envisaged: because Toulouse-Lautrec was such a popular artist, no sooner were the posters pasted up in the streets of Paris and the provincial towns and cities of France, or the local people removed them to decorate their homes.

Dr. MacCabe's team consisted of Arthur Chase, F. Pope, "Jack" Stocks, "Charley" Barden, and C. G. Wridgway. They were

Right: Fig. 2.16. The final poster, with Constant Huret on the bike behind a multi-seat pacing machine, and Simpson himself with importer Louis Bougle, a.k.a. L. B. Spoke.

all supposed to be riding bikes with ordinary chains, but MacCabe had let it be known that the chain to be used was something special, and it was not until the team came onto the track that the spectators learned that the Irish doctor had equipped his men's machines with a block chain made by the Cycle Components Manufacturing Company of Birmingham, called the "Pivot." A special feature of the chain was that each pin was pear shaped with the link rocking on the hardened point of the chainring, thus giving the smallest possible area of contact, which was claimed would reduce friction. Simpson accepted this ploy, still convinced that his chain would rule the day. MacCabe's riders would be paced by the famous Dunlop pacing team, riding triplets and quads. All the racers and sixty men in the pacing team wore dark blue strip edged in gold.

The morning of race day was bright and warm; *The Times*' weather forecast for London on Saturday was "unsettled, close, some wind; rain expected later in the day; average temperature 72° Fahrenheit" [22° C]. The forecast proved to be correct, although there was a strong wind blowing across the track, which made the multi-manned pacing machines hard to handle. As well as being a big sporting event, it was also a social occasion, so before the racing commenced, Dr. MacCabe entertained the press, his friends, and followers to a luncheon in a marquee set up in the track centre. The food was excellent, the wine flowed freely, in anticipation that the journalists would give a good report of the event. Outside the band of the Honourable Artillery Company played a selection of popular tunes to entertain the diners, and a great time was had by one and all.

Posters advertising the event had been pasted up all over London, and the daily and sporting newspapers all carried notices of the race; no expense was spared in informing the public of this great event. The Catford track was built to accommodate all classes of society. Boxes were available for persons of rank and distinction, five shillings would buy a reserved seat for the well-heeled spectator in the stand, two shillings and six pence would gain admittance to the enclosure, and the hoi-polloi could get in for a shilling. When the gates opened, the public rushed in. Within an hour, some 8,000 spectators lined the track railings, and by the time hostilities were due to commence, at three o'clock in the afternoon, another 5,000 had poured in, packing the stadium to capacity.

Before racing could begin, the riders were introduced to the public. The French contingent received polite applause, the British riders were well supported, but the biggest ovation was reserved for the "Mighty Midget," Welshman Jimmy Michael. The introductions were followed by a colorful parade of the pacing teams. By tradition, the guests, the Gladiator team, were first onto the track, resplendent in their light blue strip, closely followed by the home-based Dunlop team dressed in somber dark blue. Riding four abreast, they were an impressive and colorful sight. Although the teams should have been perfectly matched athletically, the French had an aura of invincibility about them.

It was nearly four o'clock before the pre-race overture was over and the riders for the first race in the match, a five-mile event, were on the starting-line. They were Jimmy Michael (Simpson chain) and Charley Barden (plain chain). It was considered that the two were evenly matched and a great tussle would ensue. Michael was first on to his pacers, but Barden was soon up with him, and by the fifth lap, following a quad, pulled away from his opponent and assumed a commanding lead. This seemed to affect Michael badly: he kept slowing up, and his pacers were forced to slow down so he could catch up. Warburton, his manager, called for the quintuplet to be put on, but once again he could not hold the pace. He appeared to be over-geared and completely exhausted, and having only covered some three miles, he came to a standstill. Warburton rushed over to his rider and had to help him off the track.

The spectators were stunned to see their hero give in so easily, and gave voice to their disappointment. The officials had seen Warburton hand Michael a drink prior to the start of the race and were suspicious that something untoward had transpired. When asked for an explanation for his collapse, Michael insisted that he had been poisoned by his manager and was so ill that he was unable to continue. In the changing rooms there was much talk about what had caused Michael's failure. "Jenny" Walters, a Gladiator rider, insisted that Michael had been given only water to drink, and suggested that his failure was due to "a very low method of living." Several riders and handlers claimed that his manager, knowing that he was not in good condition, had laid bets with the bookmakers that he would lose and gave him a laced drink to make sure he did not finish the race. One wag was convinced that as Michael had only been married for two months, his over-indulgence in marital coupling had

£1,000 to £100.

THE

GREAT CHAIN MATCHES.

(UNDER N.C.U. RULES).

———o———

THE SIMPSON LEVER CHAIN TEAM

v. IRISH FIELD,

CATFORD TRACK, Saturday, JUNE 6th,

Starting at 3.30 p.m.; Gates open 2 p.m.

EVENTS: 5 MILES, ONE HOUR, & 50 MILES

(ALL PACED MATCHES).

Also J. S. Johnson, the acknowledged American Champion, will attempt to lower

THE ONE MILE RECORD.

IRISH FIELD TEAM (selected from):— Messrs. A. A. Chase, F. Pope, J. W. Stocks, and C. G. Wridgway.

SIMPSON LEVER CHAIN TEAM (selected from): —Messrs. Huret, Platt-Betts, A. V. and Tom Linton, Michael, Walters and Protin.

Band of the Hon. Artillery Company will perform a selection of music.

Frequent Trains on the S.E. Railway to Catford Bridge and Lewisham Junction ; also to Catford Station, L. C. and D. Railway.

Admission to Grounds ONE SHILLING.

Reserved and Numbered Seats, 5s. Unreserved Enclosure, 2s. 6d. Including Admission to the Grounds.

Seats can be booked of the Managers—F. W. BAILY (Irish Field), 94, Oakfield Road, Penge ; J. DRING (Simpson Lever Chain), 57, Chancery Lane, W.C.

Left: Fig. 2.17. Poster announcing the Great Chain Matches, 1896.

Above and facing page: Figs. 2.18 and 2.19. Two photos from the Great Chain Matches, at Catford Track.

weakened him to such an extent that he could only manage three miles at racing speed!

Riding in the next match race was another of Warburton's boys—Arthur Linton (Simpson), the eldest of the brothers, who was making an attempt on the two-mile record. He was well paced, but failed to get anywhere near record time. There was no doubt he was tired, having been joint winner of the notoriously hard 600 km Bordeaux to Paris road race just thirteen days before. He had collapsed during that race, and was only able to continue after being given a reviving drink by Warburton.

The first two match races had been disappointing, and the crowd was restive, but were enthusiastic when the next event was announced—a one-hour race between Tom Linton (Simpson) and "Jack" Stocks (plain). Linton had recently become the first man to ride thirty miles in an hour, and it was believed that Stocks, who was in the form of his life, would give a good

THE GREAT CHAIN CONTEST AT CATFORD
THE HOUR RACE BETWEEN TOM LINTON (SIMPSON LEVER CHAIN) AND J. W. STOCKS (HUMBER CHAIN) WON BY LINTON, WHO COVERED 27 MILES 643 YARDS IN THE HOUR

account of himself and was quite capable of beating his opponent.

From the gun, both riders picked up their pacers effortlessly and rode abreast for the first three miles. Linton then appeared to be struggling, and Stocks pulled ahead, although his pacers were not riding evenly and took him up the banking several times. It was then that the Gladiator pacers got into their stride. Their changeovers were frequent and smooth, so Linton was able to gradually gain on his opponent and eventually overtake him. At a signal from Warburton, the quintuplet was put on, and Linton gradually pulled away even further, holding the position until time ran out. His distance was 29 miles 643 yards, not a new record, but it was an exciting race and a crowd-pleaser.

The next event was not part of the chain match program. John S. Johnson, the American champion, had been accompanied to the venue by his manager, the irrepressible Tom Eck. Johnson, riding a Gladiator bicycle fitted with a Simpson chain, would attempt to lower his own flying-start one-mile world record, set on the Bordeaux track in May of that year. He was well paced by two quads, but it was obvious that he needed more time to acquaint himself with the Catford track, which was unfamiliar to him. After several attempts, and despite loud vocal support from the crowd, he realized the record was unassailable at this meeting and withdrew.

The last race of the match was between Constant Huret (Simpson) and Arthur Chase (plain) over fifty miles. This event was seen by the spectators as a battle between a plucky Englishman and a tough, experienced Frenchman. They were very well matched, but once again the superior pacing of the Gladiator team negated all the best efforts of Chase, and at the finish, the Frenchman not only won comfortably but set a new world record.

We know from the sketches made by Toulouse-Lautrec that the legendary American champion Arthur Zimmermann was at the Catford meeting, dressed in racing strip and complete with bicycle, but did not compete in any races, so it must be assumed that he was only there as a spectator and to pose for the artist. Another rider, "Jack" Platt-Betts, of the Simpson team, was present at the track but was not called upon to ride, so was probably there as a reserve.

William Spears Simpson had proved to his own satisfaction that by winning two out of three races in the match that his lever chain proved it had an advantage over all other chains. The cycling press and spectators, however, were under no such illusion. The successes had nothing to do with the chain, and everything with the superior pacing provided by the Gladiator team. Before this event, the Dunlop pacing team were considered unbeatable, and as a result, the riders became complacent and confident that all they had to do was turn up, ride, and win.

Warburton had spotted this weakness and persuaded the Gladiator Cycle Company that he could get their pacers into top condition and schooled in the art of even pacing and quick changes. To the delight of Simpson and the Gladiator Company, he proved that with correct coaching, anything was possible. The Dunlop Company were devastated by the defeat and immediately put their pacers in the hands of the coach Sam Mussabini. Under his guidance, they gradually improved, and eventually regained their place as one of the best pacing teams in the world.

As a result of Jimmy Michael's conspicuous failure in the five-mile event, and his accusations against Choppy, the NCU had no alternative but to hold an enquiry. At their meeting on the 31 October 1896, the committee passed the following resolution: "The committee have thoroughly investigated Michael's riding at the Chain Matches, held at Catford on June 6th last and in connection with the conduct of Warburton and Michael generally." Simpson, Dring, Warburton, and Michael were examined, and the committee passed the following resolution dealing with Warburton:

That no permit in future will be granted to any club, nor will any races under NCU rules be permitted to take place on any track where J. S. Warburton is allowed to enter the enclosure or dressing rooms. With regard to Michael [whose licence had already been suspended by the Professional Licensing Committee], it was decided to ask the committee to re-issue the same, and this has been done.

The minutes of the meeting do not state how the investigation was carried out, nor the names of the investigators. It appears there was no appeal procedure available to Warburton, despite the fact that the committee's decision prevented him from earning a living. As the ban only applied to England, he moved his organization and riders to Paris, and wherever he appeared received a rapturous welcome from the French public, who considered the NCU had treated him disgracefully. Warburton had no alternative but to sue Michael for libel in an attempt to clear his name.

So why were the NCU so hard on Warburton? Was it because he was so successful in developing so many riders from the amateur ranks, demanding starting money from promoters, or his brash, outspoken way of addressing officials? It was probably a combination of all these things. It must be remembered that the NCU were never comfortable with professional coaches, or indeed professional cycle racing. They preferred the idea of the amateur-a clean-limbed university gentleman taking part in sport for recreational purposes, and not rough, working-class men making money from something they were good at. Imagine their chagrin when successful uneducated athletes from the lower classes became sports coaches.

Athletics had suffered from this mentality probably longer than cycle sport. It is worth noting that coaches at athletic meetings are still not allowed in the track centre, they have to shout instructions to their athletes from the stands. In fairness to the NCU, professional sport of any kind had a bad reputation, for as soon as money is involved with competition, unscrupulous people see an opportunity to make a profit. How they make it is unimportant—race fixing, intimidation, drugs, bribery, violence, almost any means has been used to achieve their aim, i.e. to make easy money.

Warburton had known Tom Eck for many years, and was well aware of his reputation as a man without scruples when it came to money. He also knew that Eck was after his rider, but he thought that the contract he had with Michael could not be broken. Warburton enjoyed a good relationship with his riders. He had taken them from obscurity, spent time and money in developing their natural abilities, and was confident that he had earned their respect and loyalty, so he was devastated that Michael would conspire with Eck against him in this underhand manner. In the interview he gave to *The Hub* in October 1897 quoted before, Warburton had reiterated how this type of situation develops:

> I have a splendid instance of this in my mind at the present time. when a rider has been brought on by an old hand in this way and has made him into a crack, that is when the trouble begins between the two. It is the money question. The pupil is inclined to kick over the traces. However, by this time each is completely at the other's mercy.

Just a few weeks after the Chain Matches, Arthur Linton was so ill that he was unable to continue racing. In early in July, at Warburton's insistence, he returned home to Wales to recuperate. Unfortunately his health declined rapidly, and he died on the 23rd July 1896, aged twenty-eight. Warburton heard of Linton's death while he was dining with friends in a Parisian restaurant. When the news was brought to his table he was deeply upset, moved to tears; he cried out, "my heart is broken," and was inconsolable.

In retrospect, 1896 had been a catastrophic year for Warburton. He was banned from appearing at any tracks in Britain, and with the loss of his two top riders, his income was dramatically reduced. For some years, he had led the life of a top impresario, travelling first class, staying at the best hotels, wining and dining in the best restaurants, and dressing in the latest fashion. He was a famous, attractive man, with money to spend, so did not lack the companionship of acquaintances and pretty women. His business compelled him to be continually absent from family and home, consequently the relationship with his wife deteriorated to such a degree that by the end of the year they were estranged and the family moved back to England. As a devoted family man, the breakup hit him badly, but being an ebullient character, he faced his problems head on, and was determined to fulfil his commitments and build up a new team of riders.

At the height of his fame, he had some thirty riders under contact, but as his influence waned, so did his riders. He still had Tom Linton, "Jenny" Walters, and Albert Champion, his son Jimmy, two Russian trackmen, and several women racers. His latest protégée, for whom he had high expectations, was Frenchman Edouard Nieuport, an exceptionally gifted young man who was not only a good cyclist but a talented aeronautical pioneer. He unfortunately abandoned his cycle racing career after carrying out experiments on the streamlining of bicycles in a wind tunnel that he later applied to aircraft.

Unbelievably, during 1897, Warburton's problems multiplied: his doctors diagnosed that he was suffering from a heart disease, and his health was in such a perilous state that he was compelled to spend time in the English Hospital in Paris. Friends and colleagues feared that his days as a trainer and manager were numbered. His income was dependent on what contracts he could negotiate for his riders, so unable to conduct business from a hospital bed, he faced penury. When he left hospital, he discovered that two of his best riders had abandoned him: Albert Champion, who had long been dissatisfied over contractual terms, had gone to another manager, and Tom Linton had been contacted by an American manager who persuaded him that fabulous money could be made by racing in New World. Convinced, he sailed for New York in late October, the end of the European racing season.

Earlier that year, Warburton, ever the optimist, had begun negotiations with promoters in America to take over a team of racing men and women to compete in events and exhibition matches when the outdoor track season began. In February, Jimmy Michael was in London to attend a hearing with the NCU, and took the opportunity to meet with Warburton to see if they could settle what had become known as the "Chain Match Affair." The meeting was amicable but unproductive, as the lawsuit was based on the allegations that Jimmy Michael had been caused physical harm by poison, and unless the charge was withdrawn, the case would go to court. Michael refused to withdraw his charge, so the law would have to take its course. The two men would never meet again.

Warburton had eventually persuaded the NCU to hear his appeal against the ban, and had traveled to London to plead his case. He lodged with the Grace family at their home in Sydney

Below: Fig. 2.20. Choppy Warbutton (top center), surrounded by some of his riders and pacers at Olympia, 1896. The ladies in the back were not merely there for decorative purposes, they too were professional racers in Choppy's care.

Road, Wood Green, and had spent several days meeting old friends and collating evidence for the hearing. On the evening of December 16th, Warburton and old cycling acquaintance Laurie Edwards, who was also staying at the house, had been out for the evening, returning to Sydney Road at about 11.15 PM, and after joining the family for a night-time drink, all retired for the night. The next morning, when Warburton did not appear for breakfast, Edwards knocked on his bedroom door. Getting no reply, he entered the room and found Warburton lying naked on the floor with a towel in his hand. He could not be revived, so a doctor was called, who after carrying out a preliminary examination, pronounced him dead.

Immediately efforts were made to inform his family, friends, and colleagues of his passing. It proved difficult to contact his wife and daughter, as they were staying with friends at an unknown address in Bury, Lancashire, prior to sailing to Australia. Eventually they were traced, and made their way to the house in Wood Green. Warburton's son Jimmy, his brother George, and his onetime star riders Jimmy Michael and Tom Linton, were all living in America. They were contacted, but would be unable to return to England in time for the funeral. Edouard Nieuport, one of Warburton's latest protégés, was in London, and on hearing of the death of his mentor, hurriedly made his way to Wood Green to express his condolences to the family. An inquest was held on the 22nd December at the Wood Green Town Hall. The coroner questioned Dr. Slater Jones who had attended Warburton as to the cause of death, and stated that the post-mortem showed that the heart was enlarged to almost twice normal size and that death was caused by heart failure. A verdict of "death from natural causes" was returned.

The coroner's officer who carried out an examination of his room found clothing, papers, a suitcase, toiletries, and money to the value of three-halfpence. The cost of the funeral was beyond the means of his family, so they were met by the magazine *Sporting Life*, with contributions from William Spears Simpson and companies in the bicycle trade. Wreaths were sent by the French sporting magazine *Journal des Sports* and from many other publication all over the world. In Paris, Albert Champion, past member of Warburton's team of riders, organized a collection from among his fellow riders that contributed toward a spectacular floral tribute sent by the magazine *Le Vélo*. Numerous letters of condolence were received by his wife and daughter, who maintained a vigil beside the coffin prior to the burial.

The funeral service took place at the New Southgate Cemetery the day after the inquest. It was bitterly cold, and most of the city was covered in a dense fog, so bad that many people were unable to make the journey. As a result, only twelve mourners gathered at the graveside for the burial service. Even the officiating minister was nearly an hour late. It was a sad and miserable send-off for a man loved and admired by so many people. He had lived a full life, and by his expertise and dedication had made it possible for several young people from impoverished backgrounds to enjoy a life of fame and fortune beyond their wildest expectations. There was enough money remaining after meeting the costs of the funeral to pay for a headstone for the grave. The simple inscription reads:

JAMES EDWARD WARBURTON
(CHOPPY)
DIED 17TH DECEMBER 1897
AGED 53 YEARS
ERECTED TO HIS MEMORY BY
SORROWING
ENGLISH, SCOTTISH AND FRENCH
FRIENDS

Right: Fig. 2.21. Choppy's grave stone in New Southgate cemetery, Section P, Plot 634, photographed by Steve Griffith in 2011.

They even got his age wrong: he was fifty-two not fifty-three. Sadly, the headstone carried no dedication from his wife and family. Was this just an omission or had personal bitterness carried on beyond the grave?

Perhaps the last word should be given to one of his legion of admirers, who wrote to the *Blackburn Standard* mourning his death, in the same Lancashire dialect as spoken by Choppy:

Choppy's gone for his long rest. He'd bed mony a spin ageon time, but th' owd scythe-bearer's run him off at last, an' other owd face hes passed away fro'us, never to return. Things o somehow's seemed to go colly west wi' him ever sin went wi' his cups an' other prizes to America. As a long-distance runner he wur beawt equal in his best days, as' th' vast number of prizes he won testified, an' nonry wur mooar popular. Lancahire wern'd fill his place in a hurry, his end were sad an' sudden.

Chapter 3.

About That Little Black Bottle

HISTORY HAS NOT been kind to Choppy Warburton. He has been called a poisoner, a cheat, and a charlatan by the authorities, the media, and the Olympic movement. During his lifetime, his "little black bottle" became his trademark and talisman. There is no doubt that he actively encouraged the myth that the bottle contained something magical, the ingredients known only to him. The illusion was successful, too successful,

Right: Fig. 3.1. This detail from Toulouse-Lautrec's original sketch for the Chain Races shows Choppy rummaging through his big bag, presumably getting ready to hand the rider (portrayed is Arthur Zimmerman) a taste of his potion.

as his reputation as one of the first and best trainers England has produced has been tarnished by the effect the contents of his bottle were thought to have had on his riders. The first recorded incident was the miraculous recovery of Tom Linton after imbibing from Warburton's bottle during the 1896 Bordeaux to Paris race, and his subsequent death a few weeks later.

Despite the lack of conclusive evidence, the incident has resulted in Linton being immortalized as the first athlete to die as a result of taking drugs in competition. He undoubtedly competed in too many races over too short a period of time, took insufficient rest, and was in poor physical condition when he returned home to Aberaman to recuperate. Soon after his arrival, he became unwell with an undiagnosed illness that developed into typhoid fever, a disease that has been described as the scourge of the over-trained. On the 23rd July 1896 he died of heart failure.

The second incident was when Jimmy Michael collapsed during his race in the Chain Matches in June of the same year. Once again, it was Warburton who had given Michael a drink from his little black bottle prior to the race, and Michael claimed that Choppy had poisoned him. It is more likely that Michael had used this ploy to break his contract with Warburton so he could go to America, where he expected to earn more money.

Both instances have been attributed to Warburton and his alleged misuse of stimulants. He was tried and convicted by the newspapers and uninformed public opinion. No official enquiry was conducted. As there were no controls on the use of drugs, no list of proscribed substances was issued by the authorities, so no athlete could be tested for illegal drug use. The only charge against Warburton by the NCU was for ungentlemanly conduct, though without evidence, and they had imposed a ban that prevented him from being admitted to any track in Britain. The ban, and the loss of two of his best riders, affected him greatly, and although he maintained a devil-may-care façade, his confidence was badly shaken, and the constant worry about his ever-declining income gradually undermined his normally robust health.

When asked by friends and journalists about the contents of his black bottle, he was vague and non-committal. During his time as an athlete in the north of England, he had known many old-time trainers who were extremely knowledgeable on the subject of herbs, their restorative powers, and pain-killing properties. Long before the National Health Service took control of their well-being, people depended on folk medicine and the services of "white witches." Every village and district had one. They could mix a concoction of herbs to cure any ailment and were often surprisingly successful. There is little doubt that Warburton knew the right herbs to use, and created a potent brew to be administered to his riders in time of need.

Whether the mixture would have passed a modern drug test is doubtful, as native people around the world since time immemorial have used extracts from potent plants and herbs to combat fatigue and give their warriors courage. In the Victorian age, when Warburton was practicing his craft, the use of drugs was socially acceptable, and indeed often encouraged. The only formality required of the pharmacist was that the customer give an explanation as to what the drug was to be used for, and if the story was acceptable, sign the poisons book, pay the price, and use it for whatever purpose one had in mind.

Laudanum, cocaine, arsenic, strychnine, caffeine, and nitroglycerine were all available from the local pharmacy to treat everyday ailments, dose athletes, or kill a spouse—which some trainers and husbands or wives did with little chance of being detected. Laudanum was widely used by all classes of society. It was an opium-based painkiller used to treat headaches, depression, and other nerve-related disorders; it was also very effective in calming fretful babies. Both arsenic and strychnine were used in cosmetics and stage makeup preparations.

Caffeine was, and still is, added to drinks as a stimulant. BikeBiz.com, a cycling news site on the Internet, reported in October 2007 that the newly introduced Powerbar contained caffeine, and goes on to explain:

> Athletes and coaches have long known that caffeine can enhance athletic performance. Caffeine stimulates the central nervous system. The advantage of this effect for athletes is that caffeine can delay the onset of symptoms associated with mental fatigue. Caffeine shortens reaction times and can help an athlete to avoid the coordination problems that tiredness can cause.

Nothing new there then. Coca-Cola, the world's most popular soft drink, was originally marketed in 1885 as a patent medicine, its magical formulae contained extracts of coca leaves, kola nuts and, as the brand name implies, cocaine. As soon as it came onto the market, Coca-Cola, with other ingredients added, was used extensively by trainers as a stimulant. During this period, a range of products appeared on the market, all claiming to give a boost to flagging minds and limbs. Cuca-Fluide, widely advertised as a stimulant and an aid to recovery, contained a substance made from fresh green cuca leaves and was available in various forms: pellets, tablets, chocolate bars, and in a liquid to be added to water, tea, or coffee.

The Pure Water Company, of Battersea, London, manufactured a bottled drink called Kola Champagne, made from kola nuts, and marketed it as a cure for muscular fatigue and having the effects of "lifting the spirit." Another product sold under the curious brand name Vin-Kafra contained an ingredient named oul, or steraculia, said to be chewed by the natives of Africa to give them strength and increase their powers of endurance.

The taking of drugs by racing cyclists and other athletes was unexceptional, and seldom mentioned in the press. So when a rider was incapacitated by overindulging in a particular substance, the press would refer to the rider's absence from competition as "on account of ill health."

Manufacturers of these products were aware of the demands cycle racing imposed on the competitors, and targeted riders relentlessly. The splendidly named Cuca Cocoa Challenge Cup, a much respected award for the winner of a 24-hour cycle race for amateurs, was presented by a company that marketed a brand of cocoa to which cuca was added, to give, as their advertising blurb explained, "an extra kick." The drink was endorsed by the highly respectable Cyclists' Touring Club, that ultra-conservative organization controlled by middle- class gentlemen who would, it must be assumed, have been horrified if they had been aware that their club was associated with a company that sold products that contained questionable ingredients.

During the late 1800s, the most popular cycle races were long, both in time and distance, demanding exceptional feats of speed and endurance from riders. Victory, or a plucky performance, could bring handsome financial rewards for both rider and manager, so it was quite normal for handlers to give riders in their care preparations to fight fatigue and pain.

ROOT'S

CUCA

COCOA
AND
CHOCOLATE.

"Your Cuca Cocoa is, in my opinion, a most invaluable beverage. It is a nerve, blood, and muscle tonic of high value. It possesses remarkable restorative properties, as I can testify to from personal experience. It is a useful 'Pick Up' after illness. Its stimulating and nourishing properties render it extremely serviceable in the lying-in room, and I can strongly recommend its daily use to nursing mothers as a splendid milk-producer. It forms a capital diet for weakly children. In brief, it is the best preparation of Cocoa yet put upon the market.

"Yours faithfully——, M.R.C.P.E., &c."

"THE LANCET," Oct. 3rd, 1891.
"This is an excellent Cocoa. In this novel preparation there are contained two substances of very definite therapeutical value- a renowned restorative and a powerful stimulant and tonic."

ROOT & CO., LIMITED,

88, Great Russell Street, London, W.C.

COCOA, in Tins: ¼lb., 1/-; ½lb., 1/11; 1lb., 3/9.
CHOCOLATE, in Boxes, 6d. and 1/. Stores, Chemists, and Grocers. Samples free to Doctors and Nurses on application.

Above and right: Figs. 3.2 and 3.3. Cuca Cocoa advertising, on a poster, right, and a display advertisement in *The Nursing Record*, of the Royal College of Nursing, June 1892 (above).

While participating in the grueling six-day races, which entailed almost continuous riding, handlers would give riders coffee boosted with extra caffeine and sometimes spiked with cocaine and strychnine, and during the night, when riders were most fatigued, they would drop flakes of cocaine on their tongues as they rode past. During the brief breaks in the racing, handlers would massage coca-butter mixed with cocaine into the rider's legs to relax tired muscles. Every type of alcohol was used and indeed recommended by medical experts—cognac drunk neat or added to milk or Coca-Cola or wine, either neat or mixed with water. They were doing nothing illegal: drugs and stimulants were not banned by the authorities, and indeed were seen as an acceptable method of boosting an exhausted athlete's performance.

Constant Huret, a close friend of the Linton brothers and a member of the Gladiator team managed by Warburton, described to a reporter of the magazine *Sporting Life* in March 1897 that when riding a twenty-four hour race, his diet comprised:

> ...one and a half pounds of chocolate, three quarts of boiled rice and milk, two quarts of tapioca, six pears, several bottles of warmed Burgundy, several bottles of Vichy water, a pint of thick chocolate, several bottles of port wine, some soup, and beef tea.

Left: Fig. 3.4. Today's body builders rely on "sports nutrition," such as these Kola Nut capsules, sold as "dietary supplements," and what many other athletes are taking is slowly coming to light these days.

The food and liquor are generally taken in small portions while riding round the track.

There is no reason to assume that this type of race diet was unique to Huret, so it must be accepted that the mixtures and quantities were the normal fare for riders in a long-distance race. Huret does not mention that he took anything specifically to boost performance or aid recovery. This is understandable because any substance taken to "aid" a rider would not be publicly acknowledged.

Unfortunately, these manufactured products, and many more of the trainers' own devising, were administered to riders by handlers with no medical or nutritional knowledge in a casual and haphazard way. Medical science relating to sport was in its infancy, and even when doctors were consulted, they had little idea what quantities of a drug could be safely used or mixed with other products, and most importantly, what, if any, were the long-term effects of administering cocktails of drugs on athletes who were exhausted and in a state of extreme physical and mental distress.

As a streetwise trainer and team manager, Warburton would have been aware of the range of drugs and alcohol being used. Did he administer any of these potions to his riders? Quite possibly, although when the two instances relating to Arthur Linton and Jimmy Michael are examined, it seems extremely unlikely that they were caused by such manipulation. One of the difficulties faced when enquiring into allegations of drug-taking is that, though the effect is evident, the administration is purposely covered up. Warburton certainly gave his riders herbal mixtures that could give a boost to flagging limbs and spirit, but he probably had no knowledge of what substances the riders themselves had ingested prior to receiving the contents of his little black bottle.

Chapter 4.

"Champion Cyclist of the World"

THE MODERN town of Aberaman was created during the second half of the 19th century as part of the industrialization of the Cynon Valley in Wales. The first ironworks and railway had opened by 1845, followed two years later by the mines producing coal to fuel the furnaces of the iron smelters. Homes were provided for the workers, and by the 1850s, the population already exceeded 1,200 and was expected to rise to 4,800 within a year. The only employment was at the ironworks or the colliery. Wages were kept low, and the only accommodation available for the workers were the low-grade houses built by the iron and coal masters.

A report to the General Board of Health, published in 1853, describes the poor conditions of the dwellings. The houses had been built in unsuitable locations, with poor drainage, leaving them liable to flooding and dampness. Aberaman did not have a local water supply; the inhabitants had to travel at least a quarter of a mile to the nearest public water outlet at Blaengwawr, so keeping body and clothes clean was a major challenge. The quality of life for the workers and their families was low. Expectations of a better life were minimal; their only escape had to be by their own efforts, and escape they did. Religion played a major role in the life of the people; the established church was accepted with reluctance, but non-conformity, as practiced in chapels, allowed working people to worship in their own manner, and through the bethels access to higher education.

Clubs were formed to accommodate every possible interest, from singing to flower arranging and pigeon racing. The hard physical labor made the population strong, resilient, and passionate about sport, both as spectators and as competitors. Rugby became the national sport, followed with almost religious zeal, with soccer and boxing following close behind. Wales is a country where hills dominate the landscape, so the high-wheel bicycle that became popular in the 1870s and 80s in the rest of the country did not become as prevalent in the principality. That is not to say that there were no adherents to these strange machines, but it was not until the introduction of the chain-driven safety bicycle that the sport of cycling was taken seriously in Wales.

Finding time to participate in sport was difficult. Everyone worked long hours, and church and chapel held influence over the population to a degree unimagined by the youth of today.

Right: Fig. 4.1. Arthur Linton on a Gladiator bicycle, presumably taken shortly after his victory in Paris–Bordeaux, in 1896.

On Sundays, the principality virtually closed down: doors of shops, clubs, and public houses remained firmly shut. Taking an active part in sport was frowned upon; even the humble cycle club run was considered unacceptable. It was for that reason that many sporting fixtures were held on the first Monday of the month, on Mabons Day. This was a concessionary holiday granted to the miners of South Wales, but only lasted for ten years, from 1888 to 1898.

In 1860, a laborer named John Maltravers Lenton and a glove maker named Sarah Male were married. They both lived in Seavington St. Michael, a village that, with its twin of Seavington St. Mary, nestled together in the soft green hills of Somerset, some three miles east of the market town of Ilminster. Later, John became landlord of the Volunteer Inn in Seavington St. Michael, where he sired seven children, John junior, William, Georgina, Ellen, Arthur Valentine, Mary, and Samuel. It was a big, noisy, close family. They loved and hated each other in equal measure, the way big families do. The Volunteer Inn was a typical village pub, spacious, with plenty of food and drink available, and money not a problem.

It must be assumed that in 1871 some misfortune befell the family, as they left the inn and moved to Aberdare in Wales, where the father worked as a contractor. The family of nine all lived in a small dwelling at 50 Concrete Houses in the town. As the name implies, the house was made of concrete, a seemingly unusual material at that time, but in fact concrete houses had been built in Wales since 1835. They were described in a government report as "Suitable for soldiers and the working class."

In 1876, the couple had another child, named Thomas, the only one to be born in Wales, thus increasing the occupancy to ten. By 1881, the contracting business was in difficulties, so John senior took employment as a gardener to colliery owner Sir Charles Elliot in Fforchaman, Aberdare, and moved his family to the town at 218 Cardiff Road. Although the three eldest children had left home, the boys taking employment in the mines, and the girl as a lace maker, the accommodation was still severely restricted.

From this very ordinary working-class family there emerged three of the finest racing cyclists Wales has ever produced. Arthur, born in 1868, and Sam, born in 1871, started out together, followed five years later by Tom. Somehow, probably by a misspelt entry on a race form, the family name of Lenton became Linton. Their remarkable story begins with Arthur.

As was the custom for children from working-class families, Arthur received only a basic education, and by the age of eleven found work as a door-boy at Treaman Colliery in Aberaman. By the age of eighteen, he had progressed to the position of haulier in charge of the pit ponies. Although working conditions underground were dirty and unpleasant, he was a fit and healthy youth, and the hard, physical work had made him strong. Away from the pit, he was interested in all types of sport. Not having the bulk needed to play rugby successfully, he joined the newly formed Aberaman Cycling Club, and by diligent economy saved enough from his wages to buy a second-hand high- wheel

Below: Fig. 4.2. This view of Abaraman Colliery was typical of the Welsh towns from which the Linton brothers and Jimmy Michael hailed.

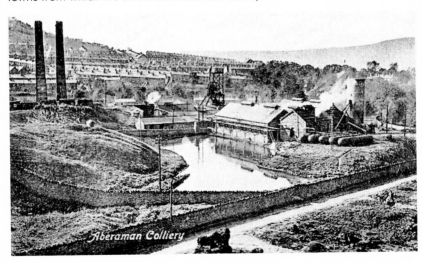

bicycle. After mastering the idiosyncrasies of his machine, he was soon scorching over the roads of south Wales, reveling in the sense of freedom and independence that cyclists enjoy.

By the early 1890s, when the pneumatic-tried safety bicycle had become popular and readily available, Arthur acquired a racing model, and was soon competing in road and track races in his area, coached by the captain of his club, Jack Jones. On the 7th October 1891 he took part in a 100-mile road race from Cardiff to Hereford and back. During the race, a storm raged, and Arthur narrowly missed being killed by a falling tree. Deciding that the Gods had spared him, and not wishing to test their goodwill further, he abandoned the race and returned home by train.

At that time, track racing was becoming popular all over the country, and five tracks had been built within easy reach of Aberaman, at Cardiff, Carmarthen, Mid-Rhondda, and Pontypool. The Cardiff track was at the Harlequins Cricket and Football Club ground, where Arthur was a member. It was one of his favorite training venues, and it was there that he set and broke many Welsh records.

By 1893, Arthur was 25 years of age. He had grown into a fine looking young man, about five-foot seven-inches in height, with dark hair and a fashionable moustache. Lean and tough, a legacy from many years' hard physical labor and cycle training, he was a man of few words, quiet, shy, dignified, and fiercely proud of his adopted homeland. He spoke Welsh fluently, and English with a strong Welsh accent that gave no clue that he was born an Englishman. He lived a Spartan existence, his only interests being training and racing, and despite being an attractive, and later in his career a comparatively wealthy, man, he never married.

On the 27th May that year, at a race meeting at the Harlequins Sports Ground in Cardiff, Arthur Linton made history by breaking all Welsh records, from five to twenty-two miles, including the unpaced world hour record, with a distance of 22 miles, 1,510 yards. The previous world record had been established by Frenchman Henri Desgrange sixteen days earlier at the Vélodrome Buffalo in Paris. But the celebrations were short-lived, as the National Cyclists Union (NCU), the sports ruling body at that time, refused to ratify the distance as a world record for reasons now lost in time. Perhaps the track size had not been officially measured and certified, or an officially recognized observer had not been in attendance. Whatever the reason, Desgrange still held the record.

Nevertheless, news spread that a new, talented long-distance rider had emerged from the Welsh hills, with the ability to challenge the best riders in the world. As a result of his successes, Arthur was invited to compete in his first event at Herne Hill in London, the Mecca of English track racing. The event was a 24-hour race for the magnificent Cuca Cocoa Challenge Cup to be held on the 21st July. There were eighteen entrants—fourteen on safeties and four on tricycles. His main opponent would be the redoubtable Frank W. Shorland, winner the previous year and one of England's best long-distance riders. Arthur showed strongly from the gun and pushed Shorland hard over the first 100 miles, but began to fade from lack of food and organized pacing.

Although he failed to finish, he impressed everyone by his tenacious and strong riding. He clearly needed expert advice and was, as the journalist of *The Cycling World Illustrated* reported: "... very green, and his attendants did not know how to feed him, and he was badly served with pacing machines." All was not lost however: the press and cycle racing aficionados were now aware that a new talent had arrived to challenge the established stars.

A few weeks after the Cuca Cup race, Arthur made another appearance at Herne Hill, competing in the twelve-hour race for the Anchor Shield. This time his principal opponents were A.W. Horton and C. G. Wridgeway, both seasoned long-distance experts. Showing his inexperience, Arthur led from the gun, leaving the field in his wake and covering the first 200 miles in just over 10 hours. It was at this point that he began to fade and was caught and passed by Horton and Wridgeway, eventually finishing in third place. On the 21st October, once again at Herne Hill, he made an attempt on the British 100-mile record. Despite numerous punctures and ineffectual pacing, he set a new record of 4 hours, 29 minutes and 39.5 seconds.

In the autumn, Arthur felt that he had achieved all he could as an amateur, and after consultation with his brothers and trainer, decided that it was time to try and earn some money from his racing and turn professional. They were aware that the best trainer in the world at that time was Choppy Warburton; so Arthur packed his bags and set off for Paris, where the coach was based. Warburton's scouts had already informed him of the Welsh rider's potential; so after spelling out the conditions of employment, Warburton put him under contract with the Gladiator team.

Arthur's first engagement was a publicity stunt arranged by Warburton to get him noticed in Paris: he was to race his bicycle against a horse ridden by Buffalo Bill at the Vélodrome de la Seine. The event was bill-posted all over Paris, and previewed by the press. The stunt worked, he was now known to Parisians as the man who rode against a cowboy! His next task was to prove his worth against tough, experienced professional racing men who had done everything and been everywhere.

During the winter, Arthur competed in a program of indoor races all over the continent, designed by Warburton to give him experience and prepare him for the hard life of a professional bicycle racer, which meant constant travel, sleeping in strange hotel beds, training, and racing. His main sponsor, the Gladiator Bicycle Company, was patient during this build-up period, but would soon be demanding results from their latest signing.

By the end of the year, Arthur was joined in Paris by his brother Tom and his protégé from the Aberaman Cycling Club, Jimmy Michael. On the recommendation of Warburton, they were both put under contract with the Gladiator team and were found accommodation at the company hostel. After being introduced to their team-mates and soigneurs, they were sent to the factory to be fitted out with bicycles and equipment. There was barely time to familiarize themselves with the Parisian tracks before Christmas was upon them.

Although Warburton was a strict taskmaster, he understood the importance of family life, and sent the three lads home to Wales for Christmas—with the stricture not to overindulge, because 1894 was going to be a busy year.

They returned to Paris late in December straight into a punishing training schedule. The intense cold and ice on the roads and tracks made training outdoors almost impossible, so all their riding was done on the indoor race tracks. The velodromes, however, were unheated during the daytime and were very cold, making the training sessions highly unpleasant.

Warburton, in his role of manager, had programmed the whole 1894 season—Tom Linton and Jimmy Michael with middle-distance races, and Arthur Linton with a series of punishing long-distance races, interspaced with exhibition rides culminating in a plan to declare him "Champion Cyclist of the World."

Professional racing had evolved without a central international body, with countries issuing amateur and professional licenses to their own riders. The NCU controlled the sport in Britain, and made some attempt to officiate at a world level, but shied away from staging a recognized world championship. The growing public interest in cycle racing by the late 1880s resulted in promoters and sponsors wanting to turn habitual winners into "stars" and "champions" as a means of improving attendances at race meetings and to sell more bicycles.

As no official championships were being organized, this led to a situation where managers declared riders in their care to be national or world champions after a series of successful publicized races. It was by this method that Arthur Linton, after two races in Paris, was declared "Champion Cyclist of the World" by his manager Choppy Warburton.

The first race in question was a 100 mile event that took place on Sunday the 14th January 1894, at the Vélodrome d'Hiver. His opponent was the French champion, Jules Dubois.

The race was expected to be hotly contested, so the venue was filled to capacity, with some 17,000 spectators, the vast majority of course being French. A huge cheer greeted the two men when they came to the line, both dressed in their national colors and emblems. For some unknown reason, Arthur was not using his Gladiator bicycle, but a British-made Raleigh with Palmer tires which he had ridden for many years. His pacing teams were steered by two Englishmen, Wheeler and Warwick, thus leaving no doubt that this was a tussle between the two leading cycling nations, Britain and France.

Dubois took the lead from the start, and held it for 20 miles. A few laps later Linton slowly began to draw level, but in the act of overtaking, the two riders collided and came crashing down. Fortunately, apart from a few scrapes and bruises, both were unhurt and remounted immediately. Soon after the incident, Linton took the lead, and Dubois, chasing furiously, caught the back wheel of his pacer and fell again. He was able to facilitate a quick bike change, and was once more into the fray. Linton was slightly ahead coming into the final bend, and with heads down fighting for the line, they touched and fell simultaneously. Helpers rushed forward and carried both riders in triumph from the track. It had been a monumental battle, and both men were cheered to the roof at the prize presentation, even as Arthur Linton was declared the winner.

A few weeks later a return match was arranged at the same venue. Once again the velodrome was packed to capacity, but the racing was less exciting than during their first encounter. For the first two hours both men rode neck and neck; then Linton had a front wheel puncture, and by the time he had changed machines, Dubois had gained a lap. Try as he might, Linton was unable to make any inroads into the Frenchman's lead, so Dubois ran out the winner. Despite this loss, Arthur was now in the eyes of his manager a world champion. Curiously, no mention of Arthur's newly adopted status can be found in British and French newspapers or cycling publications of the era. Perhaps journalists chose to ignore such inflated declarations by managers regarding their riders.

The authorities had realized for some time that the custom of awarding pseudo titles should not be allowed to continue, so during the 1892 Stanley Bicycle Show in London, delegates from Europe and North America had met to "institute a universally recognized series of world championships," and formed a controlling body named the International Cyclists' Association (ICA). As a result of this meeting, a series of amateur world championships were held in America the following year. The first world championships for professionals were held in Cologne, Germany, in 1895, where Jimmy Michael won the 100 km paced title.

A curious event took place at the Vélodrome d'Hiver starting the 31st March. It was a race held over a period of eight days, the winner being the rider who covered the greatest distance. The

Right: Fig. 4.3. Arthur Linton (on the bike) with his trainer Choppy Warbuton, presumably around 1894.

names of most of the competitors are unknown, but the principal riders were Arthur Linton, Constant Huret, and Charles Meyer. A contemporary report describes the outcome of the race:

> The remarkable event, held over a period of eight days was divided into sessions that totalled fifty hours of competition. The winner, Huret, covered a total of 1,749 kilometres, Linton second with 1,736 km and Meyer third with 1,728 km. The race provided proof of Linton's remarkable staying powers. On the third day when in fourth position he abandoned nineteen minutes before time was called for the day. The following day he was persuaded to remount and henceforth steadily recovered his lost position and went on to finish in second place. Linton was quite fresh at the finish whilst Huret showed signs of distress.

Throughout the summer and autumn of 1894, Arthur, the newly declared "Champion Cyclist of the World," together with his brother Tom and Jimmy Michael, competed in races all over Europe, riding any type of race that would pay the starting money Warburton demanded. Toward the end of the year, Arthur turned up at the Palais des Arts Libéraux to ride in a 12-hour race. It appears that he was in such poor condition that the reporter from *Cycling* described him as "chubby and in a half-trained condition." Much to the disgust of the spectators, he abandoned eight hours into the race.

It is curious that the Welsh trio were not given a nickname, for at any opportunity they would wear racing strip emblazoned with a Fleur-de-Lis and converse together in their mother tongue, a language totally incomprehensible to the people of the countries they visited.

During this period, Arthur established a new hour record, with a distance of 28 miles 500 yards, but for the second time in his life, the record was not ratified by the authorities.

As was their custom, the trio returned to Wales for Christmas, where in honor of Arthur being declared "Champion Cyclist of the World," the burgers of Aberaman organized a civic reception for him, consisting of a banquet at the Lamb and Flag public house, followed by a formal reception at the Constitutional Hall, where Mr. D. Williams, the High Constable of the county, presented him with an illuminated address that celebrated his achievements in cycling with the following words:

> ... as a resident of Aberaman your conduct left nothing to be desired and in connection with cycling you were not only ready to help others, but by example showed the younger members how much might be accomplished by perseverance and care... Trusting that you may achieve greater and higher honours in the future...

The people of the town presented him with an oil painting, and his former colleagues from the Treaman Colliery presented him with a gold scarf pin. These were remarkable honors to be bestowed on an uneducated young man from a humble background, a former colliery worker, who through his own endeavors had found fame throughout Europe. No one present at these celebrations could have envisaged the greater glory, nor the tragedy, yet to come.

After a restful and pleasurable Christmas, the trio returned to Paris, to face the grind of training and a program of racing designed by Warburton to set the world of cycle racing ablaze. But as with so many well-laid plans, reality was somewhat different. 1895 was not a good year for Arthur. He was still having problems with a damaged knee, resulting from a crash the previous year, and a disagreement with Warburton over lack of financial acknowledgment of his world champion status that almost brought their association to a premature end. Fortunately, the dispute was brought to a satisfactory conclusion by the intervention of a third party, allowing their partnership to continue.

Early in the year, Arthur was contracted to ride against Constant Huret in a 100-mile race at the Vélodrome d'Hiver, an event eagerly awaited by the public. The day before the event, Arthur received news that his mother had died; he was devastated, and intended to leave immediately for the funeral in Aberaman. However, upon hearing that the race had been widely advertised, and most of the tickets sold, he put personal feelings aside and consented to ride. Suffering under the weight of his loss, his ride lacked conviction, and Huret won easily. This sad event cemented the friendship that had developed between the two riders, and continued until Arthur's demise.

With Arthur now pronounced a "champion cyclist of the world," and Jimmy Michael establishing a reputation for beating any opponent brave enough to ride against him, Warburton thought that with the right advertising, a series of races between the two lads from Aberaman would result in a sell-out promotion. If the match could be staged at the prestigious Cardiff Horticultural Society Sports Day, it would attract thousands of people from all over Wales. Time permitting, there could also be a match at Arthur's favorite Harlequins track in November.

However, no reports of the events ever taking place can be found, so either agreements could not be reached with the track owners, or Warburton was having troubles nearer to home. Arthur Linton was very amiable and easy to work with, but Jimmy Michael was becoming increasingly difficult to handle, so possibly this was the reason the races never took place, thus denying their countrymen the pleasure of witnessing a battle between two of Wales' best riders on home ground.

For Arthur, 1895 had been a year of mixed fortunes. The loss of his mother had not only affected him emotionally, but had affected his form, so he was incapable of cashing in on his newly acquired fame as world champion. The only highlight of his season was his protégé Jimmy Michael winning a world title. Warburton was aware that, although Arthur was the consummate professional, and was always willing to compete in any race, he was physically and emotionally drained, and insisted that he took a break, went home, and only return when he felt fit and healthy.

When Warburton began working with the two Linton brothers, he soon realized the two men had totally different characters: Arthur was an introvert, not comfortable in a crowd, and would never be at ease living permanently away from home, whereas Tom was an extrovert, enjoyed company, and could live anywhere. So he handled them accordingly. Learning of the financial rewards that could be earned in America, Warburton was keen to take his team over there. He put the proposal to his riders. Jimmy Michael and Tom Linton agreed, but Arthur Linton was horrified and could not countenance the thought of being unable to return to Wales for perhaps a year, and turned the suggestion down flat. This annoyed Michael, who saw an opportunity to increase his earnings being denied because of one member of the team's reluctance to travel. Warburton's decision not to go to America would come back to haunt him.

The complete rest away from the hustle and bustle of Paris worked its magic on Arthur, and early in January 1896 he was back with the team, fit, well, and looking forward to the training and racing program that Warburton had planned for him.

But all was not well in the Warburton camp. Since becoming a world champion, Jimmy Michael felt that he no longer needed his trainer's guiding hand. Though still under contract, he was largely going his own way. Also his friendship with the Linton brothers was estranged, as he rightly considered that Arthur was not a "real" world champion.

The bad feeling was so strong that he left the Gladiator hostel and took an apartment in another part of Paris. In January, he further exacerbated the relationship by posting a challenge in the *Aberaman Times* addressed to the Linton brothers generally and to Arthur in particular, questioning the validity of his world championship. Since no trace can be found of this challenge being accepted, it is assumed that the Linton brothers treated this outburst by a petulant one-time friend with the contempt it deserved.

The first events for Arthur in the New Year consisted of a series of short high-speed races, held on indoor tracks in Paris and London, designed to build up his stamina and ease him back into competition. His first major event was a two-week long cycling extravaganza being staged at the Agricultural Hall in London, organized by the cycle impresario John Dring, beginning at 5 PM on the 19th March 1896. A special wooden track of eight laps to the mile, with high banked turns, had been constructed for the racing. A mix of the best riders from the continent had been engaged to ride, including J. A. Lumsden and Gergess. The British contingent included J. Platt-Betts, A. A. Chase, G. A. Nelson and H. Chinn. Warburton brought Arthur Linton and Jimmy Michael, together with Lisette Marton, who rode in the series of women's races.

On the second day, Arthur rode a 100-mile race, his principal opponents being Chase and Lumsden. They both rode strongly, but could not match Arthur's pace. Chase finished second, and Lumsden retired, leaving Arthur to take the victor's laurels in a time of 4 hours, 32 seconds, showing that he was back in sparkling form. For the second week, a six-day race was staged, the competitors riding continually for 24 hours, but only racing four hours, each day. Arthur was partnered with G. Baraquin, but they failed to gel as a team and pulled out on the third day, having covered some 250 miles. Although denied the satisfaction of winning, Arthur found riding at racing speeds was good training.

Arthur's next event was held on the 19th April. It was a departure from his usual track appearances: a road race, a type of competition that he had not taken part in since his amateur days in Wales. It was a new place-to-place race, designed to test the fitness and stamina of the best riders in Europe, the inaugural Paris–Roubaix. The course of 280 km went over some of the worst roads in France. It was said that the cobbled sections were the good bits.

The event was the inspiration of two Roubaix mill owners to publicize their businesses and their town, which is situated in a remote northern part of the country given over to the production of wool and coal. The idea was taken up by the cycling paper *Le Vélo* and passed to one of their journalists, Victor Breyer, to organize. Breyer was a man destined to be involved in the careers of the Linton brothers and Jimmy Michael over the following years.

The paper considered that the new race would be an ideal warm-up for the other event they organized, Bordeaux–Paris. It would be long, hard, and a test of human endurance for the competitors. It was an ideal introduction into French road racing for Linton, and Warburton prepared him accordingly.

Race favorites were the German Josef Fischer, Danish rider Charles Meyer, and Frenchman Maurice Garin, who between them carried most of the betting money. Linton was considered an outsider, as all his previous racing experience had been on the track, so he was an unknown quantity. Also taking part was another courageous British rider, now forgotten by cycling historians, R. H. "Doc" Carlisle, who had finished third in the 1895 Bordeaux–Paris.

At 5.30 AM, the forty-eight competitors gathered on the line, and at a signal from the starter, rode off, picking up their pacers some half-mile down the road. Emerging from the forest of Saint

Below: Fig. 4.4. Bordeaux–Paris lineup, showing Arthur Linton, with Choppy, and the other favorites, Rivierre and Murtha.

ARTHUR LINTON   RIVIERRE   MEYER

Germain, riding strongly and in the lead was Linton, but just after the control at Amiens, where Warburton was in attendance, he suffered the first of six falls. His bad luck continued a few miles on, when he hit a stray dog, smashed his bicycle and, although badly shaken, fortunately suffered only cuts and bruises.

After being patched up, and receiving food, drink and a rub-down, he was able to continue on a replacement machine. However, fatigue and the culminating affect of the many falls slowed him, and he was gradually overtaken by Fischer and the other favorites. When entering the stadium at Roubaix after some nine hours of racing, he was exhausted, and collapsed into the arms of Warburton after crossing the finishing line in fourth place. The race was won by Fischer, with Meyer second and Garin, the darling of French cycle racing, in third place. Carlisle had suffered a bad fall and abandoned. The following year, Garin would go on to win the first Tour de France.

Linton had exceeded everyone's expectations. At one stage of the race it seemed that he might win his first continental road race, but luck deserted him, and fourth place in such illustrious company gained him much respect among the seasoned professionals.

After the exhausting experience of the Paris–Roubaix race, Linton enjoyed several days of rest and recuperation, then continued to fulfil a series of long-standing track engagements in France. During the second week of May, Arthur and Tom Linton, Warburton, and their team of handlers and pacers, complete with the specially prepared Gladiator bicycles fitted with Simpson Lever chains that Arthur Linton would be riding, left Paris by train for Bordeaux, where on the 23rd and 24th of that month Arthur would compete in the toughest event of his career, the fearsome 369 mile Bordeaux–Paris road race.

It was the sixth edition of the event, once again organized by the cycle sport newspaper *Le Vélo*. Fifty-six riders had entered, including the previous years' winner, Charles Meyer, and the victor of Paris–Roubaix, Josef Fischer, who by his recent form had to be considered the race favorite. In the absence of Maurice

Garin, French interest was centered on two other long-distance specialists—Gaston Rivierre and Marius Thé. Once again, all the betting money was on the continental riders, but Warburton, knowing that Linton was in the form of his life, placed a large bet on his rider to win.

On Saturday, the weather was fine and warm, without much wind, and by late morning thirty-two riders were making their way to the starting line for the noon start. Linton was considered one of the outside favorites after placing fourth in Paris–Roubaix, so was in the front row with Rivierre, Meyer, Fischer, and Thé. Behind them were the cream of European long-distance riders, including three amateur's from England, George Hunt, Billy Neason, and R. H. "Doc" Carlisle from the Anfield Bicycle Club. As the race was for professionals, the Anfielders had to obtain special permission from their club to compete, on condition that they would no longer be eligible to compete in club events.

The competitors were called to attention, the starter fired his pistol, and they were off, picking up their teams of pacing tandems and quadruplets some distance from the line. The pace was fast and furious from the gun, with the first twenty-five miles covered under the hour, and the first hundred in four hours, forty-nine minutes, a spectacular pace when taking into account the appalling condition of the roads, which were little better than farm tracks interspersed with long stretches of vicious cobblestones.

Linton and Fischer were joint leaders up to the century mark, but soon after, the German met with the same fate that Linton had to endure in Paris–Roubaix when he was brought down by a stray dog. Unfortunately he was so badly injured that he was unable to continue, so the Welshman rode on alone. When darkness fell, Linton appeared to be suffering, riding on instinct alone, and just managing to hold his pacers' speed. Rivierre, on the other hand, was following a strict time schedule and was gradually overhauling him, and by the Orleans feeding station had caught and passed him. Linton was in considerable distress, and Warburton felt that he should abandon. However, Victor Breyer, who observed the incident, commented, "Linton, who seemed done up, but, with an extraordinary amount of pluck, the Welsh rider came again, and was in front when about two miles from home."

He did indeed "come again," caught and passed Rivierre just four miles from the finish, entered the Vélodrome de la Seine, and after completing the required two lap of the track, crossed the finishing line one minute ahead of his rival, in a time of 21 hours, 17 minutes and 18 seconds, some two hours ahead of the record. Completely exhausted, he fell into the waiting arms of Warburton and his brother Tom.

Almost immediately, Rivierre lodged a protest, claiming that Linton had deviated from the official route by crossing the river Seine by the wrong bridge. An enquiry was held on the Monday following the race, where both riders gave evidence. Rivierre upheld his objection that Linton had not followed the route, with Linton claiming that he had just followed his pacers and had no idea he had crossed by the wrong bridge. After an exhaustive enquiry, it was decided to award joint first place to both riders and to share the prize money equally. At first Linton would not accept the decision, but was eventually persuaded to do so by Warburton. So the official result read:

Joint First Place: Arthur Linton, England, and Gaston Rivierre, France.

Third Place: Thé, France.

Fourth Place: Neason, England.

Fifth Place: Cordang, Holland.

Sixth Place: Carlisle, England.

Seventh Place: Gerger, Austria.

Eighth Place: Bretonnet, France.

The English contingent, all amateurs, rode magnificently despite inadequate pacing, with Neason in fourth place and Carlisle in sixth. George Hunt had been taken ill during the race and had to abandon. The following day the story of the race filled the newspapers. In their articles, the French reporters correctly referred to Linton as a Welshman, but much to his chagrin, was listed as an Englishman in the results.

The after-effects of Bordeaux–Paris on Arthur were plain to see: he was obviously exhausted. Try as he might, Warburton could not get him to take time off from racing, Arthur seemed like a man possessed, driven to prove that he was indeed "champion cyclist of the world." He competed in a series of track races in France with mixed success, culminating early in June by breaking the national records for 50 and 100 km.

On the 6th June he crossed the English Channel to take part in the much lauded Chain Races at Catford track. The promotion was a major event for his Gladiator/Simpson sponsor, and the team that consisted of his brother Tom, Jimmy Michael, Platt-Betts, Protin, and Huret. The object of the meeting was an attempt to prove the superiority of the Simpson lever chain over the standard roller chain in a series of three match races and record attempts.

The Simpson chain riders won two of the three races, so the entrepreneur was satisfied. One of the biggest disappointments of the afternoon was the unexpected failure of Arthur to get anywhere near the record time for the two miles. The spectators thought it was a lackluster performance and expressed their displeasure accordingly, not appreciating how tired he was. The Jimmy Michael situation came to a head with his failure to finish his race and declaring that Warburton had poisoned him. After the meeting, the team returned to Paris to continue their season.

A few weeks later, on the third day of July, Arthur took part in the Bol d'Or 24-hour race at the Vélodrome Buffalo. It was won by his old Bordeaux–Paris rival Gaston Rivierre, with Englishman R. Williams taking second place. Arthur started strongly, but was taken ill and abandoned. It was now obvious to everyone that Arthur was ill. He had been unable to finish his last two races, claiming that he was just tired and out of form. Warburton tried to persuade him to take some time off from racing and seek medical advice as to the nature of his continuing loss of form, but he refused.

The following week he returned to London to compete in the three-day Gold Vase event at Catford track, which was held over consecutive days starting 9th July. He started the race seemingly in good form, but collapsed on the second day. He finally accepted that he was suffering from something more serious than tiredness and a loss of form, so left immediately for his sister's home in Aberaman to recuperate.

Upon arrival, his sister was so alarmed by his condition that she put her brother in the care of two doctors, who diagnosed that he was suffering from typhoid fever and transferred him immediately to the local cottage hospital. His condition deteriorated rapidly, and Arthur, sensing that he was not going to recover, and determined to spend his last days in Aberdare, discharged himself from hospital and made his way to the home of an old friend, Michael Thomas, in Cardiff Street, where, in the early hours of Thursday the 23rd July 1896, surrounded by his family, he passed away.

The funeral was set for the afternoon of the following Monday, with the burial service at St. Margaret's Church, Aberdare. Soon after midday, the streets began to fill with people, wanting to pay their last respects to Arthur and his family. The Treaman Colliery, where Arthur had worked, was closed for the day so employees could attend. The cortege left the house in Cardiff Street promptly at 3:30 PM. Behind the coffin were his father, brothers Sam and Tom, together with other members of the Linton family, then a group from the colliery and representatives from local societies and organizations. Next were members of the Aberaman and Catford Cycling clubs. They were followed by Arthur's old friends Constant Huret, Choppy Warburton, William Stead Simpson, and a group of cyclists from Paris. The only noticeable absentee was Jimmy Michael, although he sent a wreath. Taking up the rear of the procession were two bands from his home town and one from Aberdare.

At the graveside, the funeral service was conducted by the minister, the Reverend M. Powell; hymns were sung, and the massed bands played solemn music. The grave was covered in wreaths sent by family and friends, local organizations, and the cycle trade.

So the body of a great bicycle racer was laid to rest in the soil of his homeland. To ensure that he was not forgotten, his name was added to the family memorial stone in the graveyard, and through a public subscription, a splendid gold-plated lectern in the form of an eagle bearing the inscription "Arthur Linton – Champion Cyclist of the World," and a stained-glass window

Right: Fig. 4.5. Arthur Linton with his ribbon-and-flower-bedecked bike after his victory in the 1896 Bordeaux–Paris race.

were presented to the church of St. Margaret, where they remain to this day.

Arthur was gone but not forgotten: every year, until the outbreak of the First World War, flowers were sent by friends and colleagues in Paris, to be laid on his grave on the anniversary of his death. The people of the valleys contributed to a memorial fund, and one of the first events organized by the committee was a Linton Memorial Sports Day held on Mabons Day, the 6th September. The meeting was at the Harlequins Sports Ground, the cinder track being one of Arthur's favorite venues. The program was made up of running and cycle races, backed up with novelty events. The main event was an attempt on the hour record by Tom Linton, paced by a team of prominent Welsh riders that

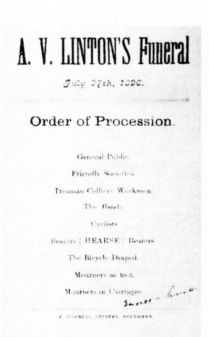

Above: Fig. 4.6. The memorial funded by Linton's friends and public donations.

Left: Fig. 4.7. Program for Arthur Linton's funeral serviced, 1897.

included his brother Samuel, mounted on Gladiator/Simpson/Dunlop pacing machines. The unbanked cinder track was not conducive to fast paced riding, so despite a brave effort, the record attempt failed.

A full program of amateur and professional races was on offer between well-known competitors to entertain the crowd, and during the course of the afternoon they were introduced to many of Arthur's friends from the world of cycling, including Constant Huret and William Spears Simpson. Displayed on a dais in the track centre was Arthur's Gladiator bicycle, a reminder of his great victory in the Bordeaux–Paris race. It was draped in red, white, and green, the Welsh national colors, with black crape around the handlebars.

When Arthur Linton died, the average weekly wage for a working man was £1. When his affairs were settled, it was revealed that he had left £24,200 to his brother Tom—not an

Right: Fig. 4.8. The stained-glass window in St. Margaret's church was a gift from Tom Linton's friend and rival on the track Constant Huret.

inconsiderable sum for the "Colliers Boy" from Wales. Indeed, he had been rewarded by riches beyond his wildest dreams, by following the path set out by Choppy Warburton only three years previously. He paid the ultimate price for fame and fortune, a fate that was to visit another member of the famous Welsh trio not many years hence.

Chapter 5.

The Other Lintons

WHILE ARTHUR LINTON was fulfilling his destiny, his younger brothers Sam and Tom continued in a less spectacular way to pursue careers as professional racing cyclists. When the three brothers started out with the Aberaman Cycling Club, Sam was considered the most promising, and he had gone with Tom to Paris to join the Warburton menage. Although he was moderately successful, it soon became clear that he could not commit to a life of constant travel and long periods away from home.

Like Arthur, he suffered terribly from home-sickness. He often acted as

Right: Fig. 5.1. Tom Linton was the youngest of the three Linton brothers coached by Choppy, and in the end the most successful.

steersman on the multi-manned pacing machines for Arthur and Tom. As he had a talent for choosing the right line during a race, he soon found his services increasingly in demand by other riders, providing a steady, if not spectacular income. Payments for his services increased considerably with the introduction of electric and motor-powered tandem pacing machines, as there were only two men to share the fees.

In 1898 he was invited to join the famous Dunlop pacing team, and in 1899 rode the Dunlop electric tandem on the track at New Brighton twenty seconds inside the mile record. As the public interest in paced racing declined, Sam's involvement with professional cycling gradually came to an end. He returned to Aberaman, to his wife Margaret, whom he had married in 1893, and their three children, Arthur Augustus (presumably named after the famed American cycle racer Arthur Augustus Zimmerman), Albert, and Kathleen, at their home at 14 Clarence Terrace. He found work as a coal miner in the town colliery, and died of acute bronchitis in March 1935, aged sixty-four.

Sam shares a rare distinction with his brother Arthur: during their lifetime, an artist produced sculptured heads of them both, and these are now on display at the Cynon Valley Museum and Gallery in Aberdare.

Tom Linton was the youngest of the Linton brothers. Born in the principality in 1876, he was the only one of the trio who could claim to be a true-born Welshman. He followed the usual life pattern of children born into poor families in the Welsh Valleys—never enough to eat, little education, and early employment in the colliery.

He was fortunate in being blessed with a robust constitution. The physically demanding work in the mine had put muscle on his young body, and the long working hours gave him stamina and tenacity, qualities he would find invaluable in his chosen career.

Following the example of his brothers, he inevitably followed them into cycle racing, and by his sixteenth birthday had built a reputation as a competent and forceful rider. He was described several years later by a journalist in the *Sporting Life* as "having the courage of a lion, standing 5 foot 6 inches tall, 38 inch chest, 22 inch thighs and weighing 129 lbs; he is a dangerous opponent to any distance rider." Unlike his brother Arthur, he was an extrovert—outspoken, with strongly held opinions, a good friend, but a bad enemy. While proud of being Welsh, he was happy in any company, could live anywhere, and did not suffer from the home-sickness that blighted his two elder siblings.

His career as an amateur was successful, but unspectacular. His inspiration was the success of his brother Arthur, who had escaped the drudgery of the colliery for the glamorous life of a professional bicycle racer. It was an example he was determined to follow. Early in 1893 his mother died; Tom, only seventeen years of age at the time, was devastated. Losing her affected him so badly that it was some time before he could contemplate leaving home to fulfil his ambition, and it was two years before he contacted Arthur's manager Choppy Warburton, and asked if he would be willing to engage him.

Choppy, who had been kept informed of his progress through the amateur ranks by Arthur, told him to take out a professional license and make his way over to Paris and that he would take him on. His first day in Paris passed in a whirl of activity, with introductions made and contracts signed, he was soon ensconced into the Gladiator system and began the hard lessons of training, racing, and learning to think like a professional cyclist. As part of his program he was encouraged to try every type of track racing, and after several successes at the distance, decided that middle-distance paced racing was his forte.

In April of that first year, Arthur took part in the inaugural Paris–Roubaix road race, and to gain experience and give moral support to his brother, Tom was allowed to be a steersman on one of the pacing machines. His riding style in such exalted company was noted by a journalist: "... he showed more enthusiasm than experience." He had no part to play in the 1896 edition of the infamous Bordeaux–Paris race in which Arthur was declared joint winner, although he was at the finish to congratulate him on a fine win.

In July the whole Gladiator entourage went to London to compete in the Chain Races. Tom was entered for the hour race against J. W. "Jack" Stocks; the pair were destined to meet in hour races many times over the coming years. Tom won the race, but did not break the record. Arthur made an unsuccessful attempt at the two-hour record; but as he was obviously still suffering from the after-effects of the Bordeaux–Paris race, failed to get anywhere near the record. It was realized, too late, that he was not simply tired, but so ill that on the 23 July he died. Tom was devastated by his brother's death; he returned heavy-hearted to Aberaman to lay his brother to rest. After the funeral, he returned to Paris, and back to the routine of training and racing, firm in the belief that work is a great antidote to grief.

The world paced hour record at that time had become a peculiarly British affair, and one that Choppy was keen to cash in on. Jimmy Michael was more than capable of successfully attacking the record, but Choppy was intent on showing off the talents of his new Welsh rider, so on the 19th June 1896, Tom and a carefully selected team of pacers assembled on the starting line at the Parc des Princes track in Paris to attack the record. One hour later a new distance had been posted, and Tom was the new world record holder. As Choppy had planned, this created great public interest in his man and subsequent press attention on "the hour" record breaking.

In October, Englishman Stocks improved the record, so Tom immediately went again, regained the record, which he held until the following year. Tom rounded-off the summer season by breaking records over 1, 10, and 100 km, and 5 miles, and won a grueling eight-day race. He had beaten the best middle-distance riders in Europe—Huret, Bonhours, Bange, Jacquelin, and Lesna. A new star was born. He was the toast of Parisian cycle racing, booked to ride in London, Paris, and Berlin. His life was full-on and hectic, and he loved every minute of it. As soon as his financial situation allowed, he left the Gladiator hostel and took apartments in Paris and Berlin.

The year 1897 was potentially a good year for Tom Linton, but it was a disastrous one for Choppy Warburton. He was ill, Arthur Linton had died, Jimmy Michael had absconded to America, and Albert Champion had found a new manager in Sam Mussabini. Although wanting to remain loyal, Tom could see that Choppy's best years as a manager were past, and he had to ensure his own future. Living in Paris at that time was an American manager-trainer, Dudley Marks, a long-time associate of Tom Eck. Aware that Choppy's days were numbered, Marks contacted Tom Linton and offered to take him on, and told him that he had been in touch with Jimmy Michael, who was keen to meet him in a series of races in America.

Although ill and living in reduced circumstances, Choppy somehow managed to keep his small team of riders together.

Above: Fig. 5.2. Tom Linton in action on the track.

Right: Fig. 5.3. A studio photo of Tom Linton. Note the Simpson Lever Chain in both photographs.

However, regretfully, the old spark and energy that had made him the best trainer in the world had long gone. Tom continued under his management, competed in, and won several top-category races, but he was fully aware that it was only a matter of time before Choppy would no longer be capable of fulfilling the demanding role of manager/trainer.

At the end of the season he accepted Dudley Marks' offer, and late in October sailed for America. Barely two months later he received a cable informing him that Choppy Warburton had died. He was deeply upset by the news, losing not only a manager and trainer who had made him into a star rider, but also a confidant and friend. Distressingly, owing to the time it would take to return to England, he was unable to attend the funeral.

The next year, 1898, saw the start of a new episode in Tom Linton's career. His new manager had found an American bicycle manufacturer and a tire maker willing to sponsor him. He had put together a training regimen programed to ensure that he was ready to compete against the best riders in the country, and if successful, establish a reputation as an exciting new rider. Soon after his arrival, Tom was interviewed by a reporter from *Sporting Life* about racing in Europe:

> Several persons have asked me since I have been in America if bicycle racing was not on the decline in Europe. Not a bit of it. I raced constantly during the season of 1897, and I disappointed my employer [Choppy Warburton] exceedingly when I informed him that I was going to America for 1898. The racing men of Europe are a great lot. They are full of fire, nerve and push, and they have all the little tricks of cycle racing down to perfection... The greatest race, all things considered, that I rode in 1897 was against the Englishman Stocks. It was for £100 a side, at Crystal Palace. In exhibitions and contest races I rode about twenty-six times last season. I raced at London, Paris, Marseilles, Antwerp, Brussels and Cardiff. At the latter place I broke Stocks' record for the hour.

In March, Tom started training for the coming season at the Charles River track in Boston. His manager had arranged for the National Track Association Team to be there at the same time to provide opposition and keep him company. A series of races had been programmed for the whole outdoor season, when he would meet some of the best middle-distance racers in the country, and victory would ensure good prize money, and eventually enable his manager to demand substantial "appearance money," thus building a lucrative career.

His first competition in the States at the end of March was at the same track, a thirty-mile race against Harry Elkes, a prominent American rider guaranteed to provide stiff opposition. The prize money was $1,300, winner take all. News had spread about this new rider, friend of the renowned Jimmy Michael and hailing from the same village in Wales, so the stadium was packed to capacity. They were paced by tandems, quads, and quints manned by experienced riders. Over the first twenty miles the lead continually changed, but in the last ten miles Tom forged into the lead to cross the finishing line half a mile ahead in 56 minutes, 50 seconds, relieved that his first appearance on an American track had been successful.

This event was followed by a series of minor races designed to bring him to peek form for his next important meeting in New York against Edouard Taylore, the star rider from France who was often referred to as the "French Jimmy Michael" because of his similarity in build and aggressive riding style. It was a 30-mile race held at the Manhattan Beach Track in June. Despite the weather being overcast, with a chilling wind, the stadium was packed with some 3,000 spectators looking forward to a courageous battle between these two foreign riders.

First out on the track were the pacing teams; each rider was allocated thirty-two pacers, all dressed in red with white stripes, to man the tandems, quints, and quads. Thunderous applause greeted the two opponents as they walked to the starting line. Tom Linton was dressed in a light-blue jersey with the Welsh Fleur-de-Lis enclosed in a wreath on the back, and black shorts.

Edouard Taylore's strip was in red, white and blue, representing the French Tricolor, confirming that the match was regarded as an international tussle.

Tom took the lead from the start, greatly encouraged by the women in the stands, who had taken the Welsh rider to their hearts. As the fifth mile was reached, Taylore's pacing machine crashed, leaving him desperately trying to attach himself to Linton's pacers. Eventually the Frenchman's pacers returned, but despite courageous riding, could not get back into contention. Tom crossed the line the winner, two laps ahead, in 55 minutes, 23 seconds, much to the gratification of his female admirers. There can be no doubt that he had an "eye for a pretty girl"—he was, after all, married and twice divorced.

The end of June saw Tom once again at the Manhattan Beach Track, this time in a twenty-five-mile race against Fred Titus, another top American rider, during a meeting organized by the King's County Wheelers. The 4,000 spectators had to endure an afternoon of storm and rain while many of the races were delayed, and had to wait until seven o'clock in the evening before Linton and Titus could come up to the mark. Tom was once again dressed in his Welsh strip, and Titus was adorned in what only can be described as a rainbow-colored jersey with black shorts.

Pacing was provided by quads and quints. As was often the case, Tom's pacers proved the strongest, and they pulled away after ten miles. The Titus pacers were so inept that he raced away from them and attempted to tack onto Tom and his pacers. He failed, however, and Tom went even further ahead to win in 35 minutes, 59 seconds, a new world record. At the finish, and during the prize presentation, the women spectators as usual made known their appreciation of the winning efforts of their hero by cheering him to the rafters.

Soon after the Titus match, it was announced that the long-awaited "niggle" match between one-time friends and colleagues Tom Linton and Jimmy Michael had been arranged and would be staged at the Manhattan Beach track. The race was widely advertised, and on the appointed day a massive crowd keen to see the race, swamped the stadium entrance. The police were called, and eventually order was restored. The three-match encounter resulted in overall victory for Tom Linton, but largely due to delays caused by mechanical failures and punctures. True to form, Jimmy Michael protested vigorously, while his adversary maintained a dignified silence.

Was it a genuine match, or just an exhibition staged by their joint manager Dudley Marks? We shall never know, but what is known is that the meeting made a lot of money for both riders and their manager. The two Welshmen met frequently at race meetings, but sadly the rift between them never healed. Jimmy Michael's belligerent nature would never allow him to forget what happened in the past. Tom Linton, who could never hold a grudge, looked at their relationship philosophically, and was content to allow the situation to continue un- resolved.

A month later, a return match with Edouard Taylore was arranged, this time staged at the Willow Grove track in Philadelphia, and once again over thirty miles. The grounds were packed with spectators, a high percentage of them women. Both men had the same pacing teams as in their previous meeting,

Right: Fig. 5.4. Tom Linton paced by a Gladiator team quad.

101

and both were dressed in the same strip. Taylore was keen to reverse the result of their first meeting, and Tom equally determined to show his complete dominance over the Frenchman. The pace of the race was furious from the gun—so furious that during the race twenty-eight new world records were set. As the duration of the race approached sixty minutes, both managers realized that if the pace could be maintained a new hour record was possible.

Taylore and his pacers understood the signals immediately and renewed their efforts, continuing at the finish line, but Tom's pacers were confused by the signals, hesitated, and could only watch the Frenchman going on to beat the hour record held by "Jack" Stocks with a distance of 33 miles, 963 yards. Annoyed by missing the chance to compete for the record, Tom surged on to complete the distance, and won the 30-mile race in 53 minutes, 16 seconds. Both men left the track satisfied with their day's work, although Tom was the overall victor over the two matches.

In August, a return match with Harry Elkes had been arranged, this time to be held at the Manhattan Beach track. The race was for the American Middle-Distance Championship to be fought out over one hour, with a cash prize to the winner of $1,200. (In those days national championships were open to all comers). It was an important event, with near perfect weather conditions, so the stadium was packed to capacity with over 4,000 spectators.

Due to the development of the internal combustion engine, motor cars and motorcycles were becoming easily available, and motor- assisted tandems were increasingly used for pacing. They were faster, which pleased the public, and as they only required two riders, that pleased the competitors, as they only had two men to pay instead of the usual thirty or so. Tom Linton's pacers were Miller and Jimmie Warburton, son of Tom's old manager Choppy. Harry Elkes' pacers were Marks and Cabaillot. Both riders were specially kitted out for the event, Tom sporting a light-blue striped jersey with black shorts, and Harry Elkes in a white jersey and salmon-colored tights.

The riders had been supplied with new bicycles, specially built for the championship; Tom's machine fitted with a gear of 108 inches, and his opponent's with 107 inches. While the pacers and riders were warming up, the band played "The Red, White and Blue" for the American, who acknowledged with a wave of the hand, but when they played "Men of Harlech," Linton responded with a salute and blew kisses to the women in the stand. Introductions over, they shook hands on the line and they were off. It was a ding-dong battle from the gun, with both men giving no quarter. However, the race was spoiled by both men having mechanical problems with broken chains and wheel changes, so time ran out with Tom Linton being declared winner and American champion.

The remaining season was taken up with races of less importance and used as a winding-down period in preparation for a return to Paris. As a result of his success in America, his manager had been able to negotiate several lucrative deals with French promoters, who were keen to match the Welshman against some of the best riders in Europe. Once back in Paris, Tom lost no time meeting up with old friends and racing colleagues and re-acquainting himself with the city he loved and now called home. By this time, he was a sporting star, well known on both sides of the Atlantic, with reports of his racing exploits headlining in newspapers in both countries.

He claimed to have won over £8,000 in prize money since turning professional, not taking into account appearance money and payments from sponsorship deals. If the £24,200 left to him by his brother Arthur is included in the sum total of his wealth, cycle racing had made him financially secure, and enabled him to fulfil his dream of escaping from a life of drudgery predestined for most men from working-class families.

For a short period of time, training took second place to wining and dining in the company of friends and pretty women. Consequently his season started late; he participated in minor races in Paris to improve stamina and give him a racing edge. His first race of the year, in April, was a meeting at the Parc des Princes where he won a race of fifty km against the American Starbuck, his old team-mate "Jennie" Walters, and Frenchman Bonhours. This was followed in May with a trip to Scotland, where at a track in Glasgow his motor-pacer lost a chain, and despite his best efforts, could not make up the time lost in fixing the machine, finishing in third place.

He returned to Paris in June for the Grand Prix International at Vincennes. The 50 km paced race was open to all-comers, and no less than thirteen contestants and their pacers lined up at the start for prizes of £80 to the winner, £40 for second place, £20 for third, and £10 for fourth. The principal riders were Tom Linton, "Jennie" Walters, Bonhours, Simar, and Champion. All types of pacing machine were employed, from electrically assisted tandems to the now almost extinct man-powered tandems and multiples.

Champion led from the starter's gun, closely followed by Tom Linton. Walters, in hot pursuit, shed a tire, crashed, was injured and taken to hospital. Racing ahead, Tom Linton lapped the field, with the exception of Bonhours, Champion, and Simar, who were desperately trying to hold his wheel. This episode brought thunderous applause and cheering from the spectators. The lead changed continually, but eventually Tom Linton pulled away to cross the finishing line alone in 56 minutes, 39 seconds, with his competitors trailing in several laps behind.

At this time public interest in paced racing had begun to fade with the introduction of motor-pacers. The sight of multi-manned machines powered by dozens of colorfully clad riders thundering around the track, closely followed by the top riders of the day was an exciting spectacle, one that smelly, noisy, motors could never replace. This lack of public interest was reflected in the reduced prize money being paid to riders.

In July Tom returned to America for an important meeting organized by the National Cycling Association at Waltham, Massachusetts, to compete in a twenty-five mile race against Harry Elkes. This meeting of the two stars of the track was keenly anticipated by the fans looking forward to an epic battle. On the day, over 10,000 people packed the velodrome. They were not disappointed: it was an epic battle between two evenly matched riders, but Tom Linton proved he was the stronger rider and crossed the line the winner in 42 minutes, 41 seconds, breaking Elkes' world record time by four-fifths of a second.

He was under instructions from his manager, that if he felt fresh enough at the finish he should continue riding in an attempt to break the world hour record. That's what he did, and added 410 yards to the distance, once again becoming the record holder. After this race, he did little racing, as the opportunity of competing for lucrative prize money was diminishing, so he occupied the time socializing with the many friends he had made in America.

In August he sailed to England to take part in some minor races, and while on the ship, received news that Edouard Taylore had retaken what Tom had come to regard as "his" record hour record. After enjoying a short break in Aberaman to

Right: Fig. 5.5. Tom Linton behind a triplet on his way to breaking the hour record in 1899.

visit family and friends, he returned home to Paris. He raced little in 1900, and the following year returned to America in a concerted effort to revive his racing career and earn some money, but regrettably few middle-distance paced races were being promoted, and his performance in the few engagements he managed to get was pitiful, caused largely by a persistent stomach upset that had troubled him since arriving in the country. Consequently, his short stay in America was singularly unsuccessful, both in terms of races and prize money, and he returned to Paris dispirited and with an empty purse.

Nothing was heard of him until May 1902, when he suddenly appeared at a race meeting in Paris, with Marius Thé riding a motorcycle specially constructed for paced racing. Tom announced that he was back to reclaim the hour record. One hour later, after riding with consummate ease and style, he posted a new figure of 68.410 km. Tom Linton was once again holder of the paced world hour record. A few weeks later he returned to increase the distance to 71.660 km, confirming that he was back in business.

Unfortunately this golden period came to an abrupt end on the Leipzig track in Germany, when both rider and pacer crashed; Thé received minor injuries, but Tom was seriously hurt, resulting in a prolonged stay in hospital. He returned to racing after a few months, but soon realized that he would never regain full racing fitness, and reluctantly had to face retirement. Fortunately he had been careful with the money he earned during the good years in America, and had enough to open a hotel in the Rue Chaptal, just off the Boulevard de Cecuchy in Paris. There he enjoyed the life of a celebrity in the city he loved until his death on the 12 November 1915. Ironically, he died of typhoid fever, the same illness that killed his brother Arthur. He is buried at Levallois-Perret.

Chapter 6.

The Fearless "Boy Wonder"

DURING THE LATE 1890s, cycle racing in America was a major sport, with a huge public following. Specialist magazines gave vivid reports on practically every race contested, and the lives of the top stars were examined intimately. The American publication *Spalding's Bicycle Guide* for 1898 made the following comments on one such rider:

> He is the most marvellous athlete the world has ever seen, for with his diminutive size he combines a

Right: Fig. 6.1. Seemingly dwarfed by his manager, Choppy Warburton, Jimmy Michael, at just 5 ft. tall, was one of the strongest riders of his time.

power and ability that is gigantic, and during the last season has duplicated in this country [the USA] his record in England, France and Germany. He has been the bright particular star of the match racing season. He has met defeat only once during the entire season, and he has met all who were brave enough to face him in a race.

So who was this rider receiving such plaudits from an official guidebook? He was not even American, but a little man from a principality on the other side of the Atlantic, Jimmy Michael of Wales.

Jimmy was the youngest son of James Michael, a butcher, and Elisabeth Tanner of Aberdare. He had an elder brother, Willie, born in 1886, and a sister, Elisabeth Ann, born in 1878. Their mother gave birth to Jimmy on the 9th November 1875, at 26 Woodland Terrace, Aberdare.

By the time he was six years old, his father was out of work, and the family were living at 27 Fforchaman Road, Cwmaman. Some misfortune must have befallen the family, because when Jimmy was sixteen, he was living with his widowed maternal grandmother, Ann Michael, in a house in Cardiff Road, Aberdare, together with his aunt Margaret, uncle Evan, and their daughters Margaret and Adellina. The house must have been substantial, as they employed a servant girl. By this time, Jimmy was working for a living, employed as a grocer's assistant in the town.

Jimmy was the first member of his family to take up cycling, and such was his enthusiasm for the sport that he joined the Aberaman Cycling Club, made the acquaintance of the Linton brothers, and had started racing in local events on road and track. Jimmy was a healthy lad, and coming from a family of butchers, he was able to enjoy meals containing plenty of meat, a luxury denied most of his compatriots. But despite this healthy diet, he suffered from a growth deficiency and never grew much beyond five-feet in height. He was, however, very muscular and strong, and throughout his life enjoyed rude health.

When Jimmy joined the Aberaman Cycling Club, Arthur Linton was already a local star. Despite being eight years his senior, Linton encouraged the lad and became his mentor, advising him on training and diet, and programmed a series of races designed to nurture and develop his obvious talent. Being so young and only having a grocer's assistant's wages to live on, Jimmy had difficulties buying a decent racing bicycle and equipment, so he had to make do with "hand me downs" passed on by club-mates. For important races, Arthur Linton would lend him his Raleigh Path Racer.

In 1894, Arthur Linton considered it was time for Jimmy to race outside the principality, so he entered him for the Surrey Hundred at Herne Hill. Anxious not to allow Jimmy to repeat the mistakes he had made himself on his first racing trip to London, Arthur organized an experienced pacing team, led by his brothers Sam and Tom, and ensured that enough food was on hand to sustain Jimmy. There were twenty-seven entrants for this classic

Right: Fig. 6.2. Jimmy Michael at the start of a race, presumably before Choppy became his coach.

Below: Fig. 6.3. This 1893 Raleigh Path (i.e. track) Racer is presumably the type of bicycle that Arthur Linton lent Jimmy.

The Little Black Bottle

race, which drew the cream of British long-distance riders. The spectators laughed when the diminutive Welshman came to the starting line—this "boy" having the temerity to pit himself against the giants of the game, such as E. and S. F. Dance, R. J. Ilsley, and C. G. Wridgeway.

From the gun, Jimmy matched every attack, and after the first hour, he was still among the leaders. By the half-way mark, he was in the lead and just inside the record. During the second-half, he had seen off all challengers, and went on to win with a seven minute margin over the runner-up in a time of four hours, nineteen minutes and thirty-nine seconds—a new record. It was a sensational win, and Jimmy Michael was lauded in the press as "the wonder boy from Wales."

As a result of this win, he was booked by the French promoter and journalist Victor Breyer for two appearances in Paris, and although he was beaten on both occasions, gave a good account of himself and made a big impression on the public and, more importantly, the sporting journalists. His next two appearances in England were disappointing.

At the NCU 50 mile championships, he started full of confidence, but pulled out after five miles, giving no reason for such an inglorious abandonment. He entered the twelve-hour Anchor Shield event with high hopes of improving on the third place taken by Arthur Linton the previous year, but unfortunately he was involved in a massive pile-up just before a hundred miles had been covered. Not having a suitable replacement machine, he was forced to retire, much to the disappointment of the spectators, who had turned up in their hundreds to see the Welsh lad beat the stars as he had done in the Surrey Hundred.

Although the 1894 season had been a series of triumphs and failures, he lost only one of the twenty-five races he competed in. This success confirmed his belief that he had enough natural talent to fulfil his dream of becoming a professional rider. During his trip to Paris, Victor Breyer introduced him to the Choppy Warburton, who, much to Jimmy's amazement, had been kept informed of his performance as an amateur, was impressed, and offered him the opportunity to ride professionally. However, there were conditions: He would have to place himself entirely into Warburton's hands and agree to the terms and conditions of a legally binding contract. Jimmy readily accepted, signed the contract, and returned home to pick up his belongings.

Jimmy's friend and mentor, Arthur Linton, who had turned professional with Warburton the previous year, was now well established in Paris, and had been joined by his brothers Tom and Sam, so he would not be entirely among strangers, and would be able to relax and converse in his native tongue. So in November, just after his nineteenth birthday, Jimmy left Wales, and after a long and tedious journey by train and boat arrived in the world centre of art and cycle racing to start his new life as a professional racing cyclist.

The first week passed in a flurry of activity, settling into the Gladiator hostel, meeting his team-mates, being fitted out with bicycles and equipment, coping with a foreign language, eating unfamiliar food, and learning how to cope with the demanding, effervescent, and overbearing Choppy Warburton. Jimmy had never lacked confidence, but being of small stature had developed a certain bombastic demeanor as a defensive mechanism. It was this sense of self-importance that would later cause a lot of grief for himself and others.

Warburton started Jimmy off with a few minor races and exhibition matches in Paris to ease him into the brutal world of professional racing and see the old year out. The next year, 1895, was to be a busy year, when the careful planning and hours of training would hopefully bear fruit. His first big test was in June, when he appeared at the Buffalo vélodrome to ride against Constant Huret in a 100 mile race. The Frenchman was a hero in his homeland, so the velodrome was packed to capacity. Huret was a tough and determined rider, and it was thought that the little Welshman would suffer an ignominious defeat at the hands of such an experienced opponent.

From the gun, the pair rode shoulder to shoulder, but after the half-way mark, Jimmy pulled effortlessly away to win in a new record time of 4 hours, 22 minutes, 46 seconds. When he crossed the finishing line, the partisan crowd were stunned into silence, but then, realizing they had just witnessed the emergence of a new star, filled the stadium with cheers and applause.

A month later, he easily bested another French champion in a race over 100 km. This was Dubois, the man Arthur Linton had competed against in 1894 to claim the title "champion cyclist of the world." A few weeks later, he crossed the English Channel to ride the Catford six-hour race, and maintained form to beat three of the best British riders of the day, Teddy Hale, Sansom Oxborrow, and Allard, together with another top Frenchman, Marius Thé. In the process, he set a new English professional record of 144 miles, 590 yards.

With meticulous preparation and a series of carefully selected races, Warburton had brought Jimmy to peak physical and mental condition. He was now ready for the most important race of his life: the first official world championships. The championships were held in Cologne, Germany, starting on the 18th August, and Jimmy had been selected to ride for Great Britain in the 100 km paced event.

When his selection had been confirmed, Warburton programmed a series of races that would maintain his form up to the championship races. Competitors all used their own pacing teams, so Warburton, leaving nothing to chance, ensured that the sixty-odd men in the Gladiator pacing team were in top physical condition, with their pacing smooth and changes slick.

The weather for the races was warm, with little wind, ideal for paced racing. The velodrome was packed to capacity every day, the spectators, mostly German, were accustomed to paced races being controlled by the top riders holding back until the final laps, then sprinting to the finish. So they were astonished by the ferocious pace set by the Welshman. Jimmy won the heats with ease, and in the final came up against the best paced racers in the world. In imperious form, Jimmy lead from the gun, dominated his opponents, and crossed the finishing line in 2 hours, 24 minutes, 58 seconds—almost 12 laps ahead of Henri Luyten of Belgium and Hans Hofmann of Germany.

The crowd responded to the spectacular riding with thunderous applause. They loved the new champion and his peerless display of athletic ability. It was a great win for the team and a triumph for Jimmy Michael, now the first official professional world champion. The press lauded his achievement, that at 18 years of age he was the youngest world champion ever. (Neither Jimmy nor Warburton corrected the error, because he was in fact 20 years old). The pair had capitalized on his small stature and youthful looks to create the myth of the boy champion.

The German rider Walther Rutt, many years after retiring from the track, related this story to the magazine *American Bicyclist and Motorcyclist*:

> I saw Jimmy Michael win that first Championship at Cologne, when he was only 18 [sic.]. I was 12 years old at the time. I remember telling my father when I returned home from the races that a "boy" had won the world's paced championship! He was 18

Right: Fig. 6.4. Jimmy Michael with Choppy, 1895.

years of age on that day [another myth: Jimmy's birthday was in November] and looked like a little boy.

Despite being one of the best riders in the world at the 100 km distance, he did not retain the title the following year, nor indeed in 1897 and 1898, the title going to his main British opponents Chase, Stocks, and Dick Palmer respectively.

Jimmy Michael returned to Paris in triumph, and for the remainder of the year took part in a series of races in the capitals of Europe planned by Warburton to show off his new champion. The races were little more than exhibition rides to familiarize the public with his name and maximize his earning potential.

The champion, accompanied by his manager, attended numerous receptions and dinners held in his honor. These events, although well-intentioned, exposed the naive young Welshman to quantities of unfamiliar food and endless supplies of alcohol. Warburton, a canny old teetotaller and non-smoker, did his best to control the appetites of his young charge, but Jimmy was already challenging his manager's control over him. Perhaps this was the beginning of a problem that was to haunt his future life and contribute in no small way to his eventual demise. The year 1895 was Jimmy's most successful of European racing. He rode 28 races, winning 22, including a world championship.

So what was the secret of his success? Without doubt he was born a champion. Athletic ability was in his genes. He was born in one of the unhealthiest districts in Wales, where coal dust from the mines covered everything, but Jimmy was lucky: he did not have to become a collier, and his family could afford adequate nutrition.

Despite his hormone-related growth deficiency, his physical statistics show he had an athletic build (dimensions in inches): Chest, normal 34, expanded 36; waist 28; biceps 11; forearms 9½; thigh 19; calf 12½; neck 14. His racing weight was 103 lbs.

When first under Warburton's tutelage, regular sessions in the gym with dumbbells and weights on pulleys built up his core strength. The majority of his cycle training was done on the track, where much attention was given to posture, pedaling style, and finding the most suitable gearing. In his amateur days, he used a gear of 65 inches. Warburton considered this much too low for paced riding, so as his strength developed, so did his gearing—through 70, 77, 80, 95, and ultimately to 112 inches.

In an interview in the *New York Times*, Jimmy described an average day:

> I get up in the morning between 7 and 8 o'clock. I breakfast on mutton chops, fruit and tea. I then take a good road ride, longer or shorter as my weight goes up or down. I dine at 1 o'clock in the afternoon. I have roast beef or mutton, tea and fruit. I never eat pastry. For supper my bill of fare is practically the same thing. My track work is done in the afternoon. I ride 10 or 15 miles at a good speed. I have no time to go round in the evenings. I don't go to afternoon teas, and I have no time for society. I don't smoke. I don't drink. I take a glass of ale with my meals occasionally. I sleep about nine hours a day.

A description of his feelings during a race was given to a reporter of the *Chicago Tribune*:

> I am nervous at the start of a race, but once the pace was set all nerves disappear, I just settle down over the handlebars and focus my eyes on the rear wheel of the pacer and try to get as close to it as possible. I shut out as much of the world as I can, pedalling where the pacer leads, high on the straightways, down the curves, rising and falling, much like a bird. During the first few miles I can hear my trainer calling out the times and giving advice, but later the only sound I can hear is the purr of the tires.
>
> After about twenty-five miles I lose all power of hearing and feeling and get the sensation that I am motionless and my actions become instinctive. As the pacers come and go I just follow them, not really aware that I am changing from one to the other. I ride almost upright, never turning my head; my upper body is held still, only my legs move with mechanical precision.

In the early part of his career, he raced with a toothpick stuck in his mouth, which he claimed helped him breathe more easily. Whatever the reason, it became his trademark. Toulouse-Lautrec included the toothpick in his first version for the Simpson Chain poster, so the image of Jimmy crouched over his handlebars in racing mode with a toothpick in his mouth has been passed down to posterity.

In the spring of 1896, Jimmy returned to London to make an attempt on the world hour record at the Wood Green track. All the preparations had been made. Warburton had once again meticulously prepared the pacing teams, had spare bicycles placed around the track, made sure the officials and timekeeper were engaged. Nothing was left to chance. The event was well advertised, ensuring that a capacity crowd of 20,000 people had paid to see the new world champion blast the record to pieces.

Unfortunately, their day was ruined, and their money ill spent, because the champion rode without conviction. Seeming but a shadow of his former self, he failed to get anywhere near the record. Was this just a matter of loss of form or was something more sinister afoot? Early in March he returned to Aberaman for two important events.

The first was a civic reception given by the townspeople in his honor, where he was presented with an illuminated address that included the wording: "Jimmy Michael Esq., Champion Cyclist of the World." Though he appreciated the honor, he bridled at the fact that a similar reception had been given to Arthur Linton when he was merely acclaimed world champion by his coach, whereas he himself had competed in a series of races for his official title. On the 25th January, an extraordinary statement had been published by the *Aberaman Times*: "We have received the following letter from Jimmy Michael with reference to the question as to who is the middle-distance champion cyclist of the world":

Seeing that Tom Linton has been boasting in the South Wales papers that he can beat me, and that he would be willing to ride me any time, and also that his brother Arthur was champion of the World, I will ride either of them, and will give them two laps in 100 km, three in 100 miles, or four laps in six hours for £100 a side and all gate receipts, race to be ridden at Buffalo or Winter track in Paris. I have deposited £20 with *Sporting Life*, so all they have to do is cover it and they can be accommodated at once, or give over talking. Anyone else in the world can be taken on the same terms, as I am middle-distance champion of the world not A Linton. I am &c., Jimmy Michael, 19 Avenue Phillipe le Boucher, Neuilly, Paris [the Gladiator hostel and training HQ].

By the time this letter was written, Jimmy had fallen out with Warburton and had taken an apartment in another part of the city. This animosity soured the relationship with the Linton brothers and his manager, and as they were part of the same team and rode the same events, the atmosphere at trackside was somewhat strained.

The second event was a personal one: on the 13th March he was married to his childhood sweetheart Fanny Lewis. They had met as children, when her father, David Lewis, a cattle dealer from Aberdare, used to deliver meat to his father's butcher's

Right: Fig. 6.5. Jimmy Michael boarding a train from Paris with Choppy. The lady on the train is thought to be Mrs. Michael.

shop, and Fanny would tag along. Their whole family had become interested in cycling ever since Jimmy had become involved in the sport. The Aberaman Cycling Club had formed a section called the Aberaman Ladies Cycling Club, with his cousin Margaret as Captain and his fiancée as Treasurer.

The marriage was solemnized at the Register Office in Cardiff. Jimmy was aged 21 and the bride 19. At the time of the marriage Jimmy was living at 4 Augustus Street, Cardiff, away from his family and friends in Aberaman. Four days after the wedding, Jimmy was compelled to leave his new bride in Wales and travel to London to take part in a 10-mile race at the Agricultural Hall, where Warburton had committed the team to ride, with Arthur Linton in two long-distance events and Lisette Marton in the ladies races.

Jimmy won his race, rather in anger than ability, and left immediately for Paris, where for three months he competed in a variety of events until the whole Gladiator/Simpson team returned to London in June to ride the five-mile race at the Chain Matches at Catford track.

The true facts of this strange affair came to light sometime later. They involved not only Jimmy Michael and Choppy Warburton, but a third party, the wily American manager and trainer Tom Eck. Although the meeting achieved its object for the Simpson Chain Company, Jimmy's actions during his race were to have a catastrophic effect on Warburton's life and fortune. It also led Jimmy Michael on the path that would eventually lead to his ignominious demise.

Under the terms of his contract, half of Jimmy's earnings went to his manager. In the beginning of his career, this arrangement was acceptable, but when he became world champion, he wanted a larger share of the spoils, and he felt that he no longer needed tutelage, so a parting from Warburton was inevitable.

Some time prior to the Chain Matches, Tom Eck had brought an American team of riders to England, and had arranged a meeting with Jimmy Michael with the express goal of taking him to America, where the public would pay "big bucks" to see their champion riders compete against the "Mighty Midget." He guaranteed that Jimmy would earn sufficient money to enable him to live the life of a sporting gentleman and see him through to a comfortable retirement.

Eck had the contract between Michael and Warburton checked by lawyers, who advised that it would be expensive to terminate, and the only possible way to get it rescinded was for Jimmy to accuse Warburton of attempting to cause him physical harm, and if possible make the allegation in front of a witness. The ideal venue would be the Chain Races, where thousands of people would be present, including NCU officials. The deception was carried out: Jimmy dropped out of the race, claiming Choppy had poisoned him. The officials took notes, and the reporters saw the incident as good copy, made mountains out of molehills, and followed the old popular-press adage, "never let the truth get in the way of a good story."

Jimmy Michael and Choppy Warburton were no longer on speaking terms. Both went their separate ways. Travel arrangements had already been made by Eck for Jimmy to sail to America, so on the 26th August 1896 he boarded a ship in Liverpool bound for New York. On the passenger list his age was shown as 20, occupation cyclist, and marital status single [though in fact he was 21 and married].

Jimmy was setting out for a new life in a new country alone. Certainly lack of money may have been an issue, but perhaps leaving a wife of just six weeks behind suggest that the couple's problems went deeper than just financial.

Arriving in America after nearly two weeks of travel and inactivity, Jimmy was impatient to get his new life underway. He was met at the dock by Eck, who whisked him away to a hotel to explain what was in store for him. Eck had secured sponsorship deals with Arnold Schwinn & Co., one of the leading bicycle manufacturers in America, and with Morgan & Wright, the Chicago-based tire manufacturer. Jimmy was happy with the financial package Eck had put together, for in addition to receiving salaries from both sponsors, he was guaranteed additional income from start money and bonuses for winning and record breaking. All he had to do was prove that he was the best paced rider in the New World.

Jimmy's first race on American soil was an hour race, a competition to determine who could ride the most miles within the time. His main opponent was the home rider Frank Starbuck. Paced riding was a new discipline for Starbuck, but he ran Jimmy close. However, he could not match his fierce pace in the final laps, so the Welshman rode out the time as winner in a new American record of 27 miles, 690 yards.

After a series of exhibition races designed by Eck to introduce Jimmy Michael to the American public, the next major event was in October at the newly opened Garfield Park track in Chicago. The oval cement track had been built for speed, and several national records were expected to fall during the meeting. The major races of the day were time trials—John S. Johnson in the mile and Jimmy Michael in the five mile. Both riders were sponsored by Schwinn, who also built the quintuplet pacing machines that were being used for the first time. Both riders were successful, Johnson setting a new record of 1 minute, 40 seconds for the mile, and Jimmy with 9 minutes, 38 seconds for the five-mile race. The 25,000 spectators who filled the stadium were impressed, and so was Arnold Schwinn, who called it a "good day's work."

During October, a consortium of cycle racing promoters in Australia contacted Eck with a substantial financial offer to take his whole team, including Jimmy Michael, John S. Johnson, complete with pacers and machines, "down under" for the winter season. However, for reasons unknown, the offer was never taken up. The old year ran out with many more successful results.

The sponsor and Eck were pleased with the impression their new rider had made, but the relationship between manager and rider had quickly become strained. Jimmy was of the opinion that he no longer needed coaching. He considered he had enough knowledge to organize his own training program; all he required was a manager to negotiate contracts, deal with promoters, and take care of the money.

To make matters worse, Eck had to postpone a series of races planned for the 1897 season because Jimmy had been called back to England by the NCU to answer charges that he had failed to honor a contract the previous year to ride a series of races in Leeds, and the legal machinations of the "Warburton Affair" had yet to be settled. Failure to attend the NCU hearing would result in his racing license being suspended in Europe and America.

He commented to a reporter of *Sporting Life:* "... that he would return to America within the next four weeks and train in the south under different management, and will be willing to meet Mr. [Tom] Linton or anyone else." Jimmy returned to America early in 1897, accompanied by his wife. He announced that they were planning to buy a house in Chicago, but in the meantime Fanny would stay with relatives in Pittsburgh. Before leaving America, Jimmy had engaged a new manager, Dave "Shiny

Below: Fig. 6.6. Jimmy Michael behind motor-pace. He is riding a specially designed bike with smaller front wheel to get closer to the pacer (see also Fig. 6.10).

Eye" Shafer, a man with vast experience of the bicycle racing world, who, unlike Tom Eck, was willing to look after the business side of racing and leave the Welshman to set his own training schedules.

In May they traveled south to Savannah, Georgia, where a training camp had been set up to take advantage of the warmer climate there. The racing program started in June with a 15-mile race at the Charles River track in Massachusetts against Eddie A. McDuffe of Boston, a formidable rider known as the "Road King" for his successes in road races. The stadium was filled to capacity, with some 20,000 spectators all looking forward to a hard fought battle. The pacers were in fine fettle, riding a triplet for Jimmy and a sextet for McDuffe.

For the first two miles, both competitors maintained a moderate pace, but by the thirteenth mile both had wound up the speed and were riding shoulder-to-shoulder, driving the crowd into a frenzy of excitement. They maintained this position until the last lap, when Jimmy pulled ahead to win by a few yards, beating the existing record to boot. At the finish, both riders were in good condition, but the extreme efforts put in by McDuffe's pacers caused five of them to collapse after crossing the finishing line.

The following two months were taken up with minor races and exhibition rides. The next major event was a series of races held at Hampden Park, in Springfield, Massachusetts, from the 14th to the 16th September. All the top riders were there—Eddie Bald, Tom Butler, John S. Johnson, "Major" Taylor, and Lucien Lesna. On the second day, Jimmy was down to ride against Lesna, the Swiss rider, in a much-anticipated 20-mile paced race.

Prior to the start, both riders and their pacers paraded around the track. Lesna and his team were decked out in an all crimson strip, while Jimmy and his men were all in black with a white stripe running up the back of the jersey and down each leg. Both received thunderous applause from the 12,000 capacity crowd. It was a "ding-dong" battle throughout, with Jimmy eventually winning by half a lap.

The following day, Jimmy was to make an attempt on the American ten-mile record that had been set by him in New Orleans some time before. The attempt was successful: new times were set, not only for 10 miles, but all the distances in between. On the 9th October at the Willow Grove Park, in Philadelphia, Jimmy set a new hour record of 32 miles, 652 yards, paced by a crack team of pacers mounted on two sextuplets, three quadruplets and a quintuplet.

This was a clear sign to all his opponents that he was in the form of his life. Two days later he was in Vailsburg, New Jersey, for a ten-mile exhibition ride. Although he had sixteen experienced pacers at his disposal, Shafer denied it was a world record attempt, but just a workout, as Jimmy had no important race commitments until December. Shafer told a reporter from the *New York Times*:

> You may see him in 15 or 18 races during the winter. I stand ready to match him against any rider in the world for races at 25, 30 and up to 50 miles. We wanted a six-hour race with Rivierre [joint winner with Arthur Linton of Bordeaux–Paris in 1896], but the Frenchman was not willing to accept our terms. For such a race it would take fully 120 pacemakers to give Jimmy Michael the pace he wants; they would cost nearly $3,000. Shafer added, big purses will be a feature next year; I believe I could offer a purse of $10,000 for a race with Stocks, Linton, and some Americans.

This statement shows that the old animosity toward the Lintons remained, and that Jimmy felt himself superior to Tom Linton. The last event of the year for Jimmy was a match against Arthur Adalbert Chase, one of the best English middle-distance riders. The race would be part of the supporting program during the popular Christmas six-day race at Madison Square Garden in New York. The event was well advertised, and some 7,000 spectators were expected to fill every seat. Their race, over 30 miles, was expected to be keenly competitive and produce some world-beating times.

Whatever the result, both men would receive substantial rewards for their efforts, as a sum of $2,500 was guaranteed. The prize purse offered was 40% of the gate takings if under $8,000, the winner taking 25%, the loser 15%. If the takings were over $8,000, the winner's percentage would increase to 30%, with the loser still getting only 15%. Their appearance on the track was accompanied by prolonged cheering. Jimmy was dressed in a totally white strip with the Fleur-de-Lis emblazoned across his chest, Chase in a strip consisting of a light blue jersey with crossed British and American flags on the back, twinned with dark blue shorts. Both pacing teams were made up of top-class riders. Curiously, Chase's team included James Warburton, son of Jimmy's former manager, Choppy Warburton, who had died a few days before the race. On account of the distance and time it would take, both men were unable to attend the funeral in London.

The manager's concern that the ten-foot high banking on the track would prove problematic for the pacers would turn out to be prophetic later in the race. As the starter's pistol sent the two men on their way, Jimmy jumped into a lead, but only half a lap had been covered before Chase was brought down by Jimmy's pacing tandem crossing his path. After a short delay caused by a heated exchange of words between Shafer and the referee, the race restarted.

Chase never seemed to recover from his fall, and Jimmy led the race until the fifteenth lap, when one of Jimmy's tandem pacers, riding slowly on the banking waiting to pick him up, slipped and crashed into a heap, just as he reached the turn. Jimmy hit the tandem, was hurled up in the air and struck Shafer, who was trackside, knocking him unconscious. Jimmy crawled out from under the wreckage with a deep gash over his right eye, but was otherwise unhurt.

The race resumed, but at the twenty-eighth mile, Jimmy touched his pacers' rear wheel, and was thrown over the handle-bars. Miraculously still in one piece, he remounted and completed the thirty miles in 64 minutes, 3 seconds by himself.

Chase was so stunned by the dramatic crashes that his manager refused to let him complete the distance.

The Christmas event at Madison Square Garden, in New York, was immediately followed by another meeting in January at the same venue, where Jimmy rode in a twenty-five-mile paced race against the latest sensation, seventeen-year-old Edouard Taylore, who was feted as the "French Jimmy Michael."

The match had been eagerly awaited, and as soon as the ticket office opened they were inundated with people wanting seats. The crush was so intensive that a detachment of police were called to control the crowd. By the time the racing started, nearly 10,000 packed the stadium.

The preliminary races created little interest for the spectators, and they were very subdued, but the entrance of Michael and Taylore was greeted with thunderous applause and cheering. Jimmy's pacing machines were a mixture of tandems and

Right: Fig. 6.7. The "Mighty Midget" grown up, so to speak. Though physically no taller than before, Jimmy Michael had gained much, perhaps too much, in self-confidence. In fact, he had become quite recalcitrant, which led to disputes, first with Choppy, and later with his other managers, the Linton brothers, and eventually almost anyone else who came into contact with him.

triplets, manned by a crew of top riders, including his friend Charles Murphy, (later known as "Mile a Minute" Murphy for being the first man to ride at 60 miles per hour, behind a railway locomotive). Taylore used only tandem pacers. His team included a trio of Englishmen—James Warburton and the Chase brothers.

At the starting line, Jimmy was dressed in an all-white strip, his talisman toothpick between his teeth. Taylore appeared in a red and white quartered suit, and had the customary pebble rolling around in his mouth. Taylore won the toss and took the inside lane. Probably for the first time since riding in America, Jimmy did not lead from the gun, and had to take second place for the first few laps. But then, seemingly without effort, he gradually overhauled the Frenchman, who was already showing signs of distress holding the relentless pace, and after ten miles was suffering badly.

The Welshman, however, was in great form, and was soon four laps ahead. By the fifteenth lap, he was only thirty seconds behind the world record. From then on, the lead changed repeatedly right up to the bell lap when, with a final burst of speed, Jimmy crossed the line the winner, with the Frenchman thirteen laps behind. A journalist from the *New York Times* reported:

> It was the hardest race Michael has ever ridden in America, and although he was more than a mile ahead at its conclusion, the pain-distorted features of the triumphant Welshman testified how fiercely the contest had told on him. Instead of the smiling walk to his quarters seen after former victories, he limped spiritlessly to receive the attention he deserved.

For their efforts, Michael received $1,500, and Taylore $1,000.

In 1898, Jimmy Michael was still only 22 years of age, but no longer considered a "boy wonder." He had developed into a mature and confident racing cyclist. However, he had been racing continually for over seven years, and the physical and mental strain of competing at such a high level was beginning to have an adverse affect on his life. The constant travel involved, and the continued absence from his wife, caused problems in their marriage. So much so that the couple had abandoned thoughts of buying a house in America, and his wife had returned to her family in Wales.

Jimmy had many acquaintances but few friends. He had a difficult personality that discouraged people from getting close to him. Even the Linton brothers, who had known him as a boy in Wales, were victims of his verbal abuse. Tom, the laid-back, easy-going one, shrugged his shoulders and ignored him; but Arthur, being more sensitive, was extremely hurt by Jimmy's continual insistence that he was not a world champion.

Early in 1898 Jimmy was joined in America by his brother Willie, who was also a racing cyclist and had been brought over from Wales by Jimmy's one-time manager Tom Eck. It should have been a joyous reunion, but Jimmy hardly acknowledged his presence, and left him to make his own way on the racing circuit. In March, when in Chicago, Jimmy took out naturalization papers to become an American citizen. He did not consult his wife before taking this momentous step, but merely informed her of his actions by cable. Jimmy was always reluctant to talk about his matrimonial affairs, but an article published on July 6th 1899 in *The Cycle Age and Trade Review* clarifies the reasons for his reluctance. Headlined "The Mystery of Michael," it went on:

> While the private affairs of the midget concern himself and not the public, the very fact of his sphinx-like silence regarding his matrimonial affairs has kept alive and the curiosity of the public in a ferment. No one knew why he should be so reticent about the matter, but it now develops, according to his wife's plea for divorce for desertion that he secretly married her in Cardiff in 1896, believing at the time that she was to inherit some $50,000 upon coming of age and upon learning his mistake sailed alone for America in 1897. Upon these charges the London court

granted Mrs. Michael an absolute divorce.

After the break-up of his marriage, Jimmy reverted to the traditional nomadic lifestyle of a professional racing cyclist, living out of a suitcase in lodgings and hotels wherever race meetings took him. As the majority of his racing was in New York, he did maintain an apartment at 629 Sixth Avenue in the city that he could call home.

The situation gave him cause to reflect on his future, and he recalled conversations he had with the old French champion Fernand Charron when he lived in Paris. After retiring, Charron had taken an interest in horse racing and had persuaded Jimmy that he had the ideal physique and mental toughness to become a jockey, and if successful could earn big money. This conversation stuck in Jimmy's mind, and early in the year he announced that he would retire from cycle racing and become a jockey.

In February he went to New York to see horse owner Phil Dwyer, who agreed to teach him how to become a jockey. Dwyer insisted that he should learn the trade from the bottom up, and Jimmy found himself mucking-out stables, cleaning harness, and running errands for the senior jockeys. To his credit, he stuck to the task and did the lowest and most menial work without complaint. Jimmy's decision to become a jockey came as a shock to his manager, Dave Shafer, who had him under contract for the coming season. It appears they had been talking about horse racing with an equine journalist, and about the success and wealth of the jockey Tod Sloane, when it was first suggested that Jimmy had the ideal build for a jockey.

Talking later to a friend, Shafer remarked "I laughed and banished all thoughts of the matter from my mind. He has by his foolishness already thrown $15,000 in sure contracts in the gutter." When asked about Jimmy's earnings, Shafer replied:

I paid to him over $18,000 as his share. This year he could have got a $30,000 backing in [tire makers] Morgan & Wright's office alone; but he got on his hind legs with Bill Herrick and now Morgan & Wright are through with him. It was they who made him, they who got me to give up the schemes I had on hand to handle him. As for my own profits, let me tell you that I have been in this business since 1893 and in 1897 I made less clear profit than any year since I have been at it.

I spent many months perfecting Jimmy and advertising and making him as he is today; the greatest drawing card in the world, no actor or pugilist excepted. Billy Brady would give $100,000 for a man to beat Michael. This shows his value. I counted to make enough money for Jimmy in a few years for him to smoke a cigar and rest the balance of his life... Today I'll bet Michael has more money in the bank than Tod Sloane.

The April issue of *The Cycle Age and Trade Review* carried the following interview with Jimmy on the subject of his conversion to horse racing:

I shall keep right on riding horses for two months yet. It is not my intension to get into condition for cycle racing until late in June and I shall be doing nothing but cycling in July, August and September. The three months will close my career as a wheelman. My three months with the horses will be preparatory to my future career, for I intend to retire the first of next October and devote my energies to horse racing only. Under no circumstances will I [cycle] race indoors for that is too hazardous and the money made is not in keeping with the chances taken... I shall not forget how to make the pedals go round while straddling horses.

During this period, the world of paced racing changed forever with the introduction of the mechanically powered pacing machine. The cumbersome, man-powered, multiple-seated machines were gradually being replaced by tandems fitted with electric motors, and in 1898 the first internal-combustion-engine pacing machines were brought to America by Frenchman Henry Fourier. As a result, racing became even more dangerous, because the tracks were not built to cope with the increased speed, and the pacers and riders wore no protective clothing or helmets, so Jimmy's inclination to seek alternative employment was understandable.

To alleviate the risk he employed Arthur Stone as his chief pacemaker, riding both the motor-assisted tandems and the new custom-built motorbike pacers. In June the long awaited face-to-face contest between Jimmy Michael and Tom Linton had been arranged by Dave Shafer, who managed both riders, in a series of three races to be staged during meetings at the Manhattan Beach track in New York City.

The duel between the two men had been widely played up as a gladiatorial contest not to be missed, and the public responded by swamping the stadium. It was estimated that some 15,000 people attended every meeting, so keen were they to witness the battle between these two giants of the track. The first encounter ended unsatisfactorily, as Jimmy punctured and lost several laps before getting a replacement machine, so

Left: Fig. 6.10. Jimmy Michael riding the special stayer machine with smaller front wheel and a big gear designed for motor-paced racing.

consequently Linton was declared the winner. It was a decision that prompted Jimmy to declare that "Tom Linton would never beat me in a fair race."

During the series, Jimmy appeared overweight, out of condition, and ill at ease, not at all his usual ebullient self. The following week the pair met again in a race over twenty-five miles. The bookmakers were there in force, and betting was 5 to 4 on Linton, although by the start it was even. It was an even, well-fought battle, with first one leading, then the other, and in the end Jimmy finishing just ahead. As soon as he dismounted, the crowd rushed onto the track and carried him shoulder-high to the dressing room.

On the day of their third encounter, the crowd outside the stadium was so large that the police had difficulty in controlling them, but by the time the two men appeared on the track, order had been restored. The betting was 10 to 8 for Linton, despite Jimmy being the declared favorite. The race was once again over twenty-five miles. After the first mile, Jimmy was in the lead, but at three miles he punctured and lost three laps while waiting for a wheel change. He suffered further delay at eighteen miles when his pacing machine lost a chain and was unable to make up the lost laps. In the end Linton, much to Jimmy's disgust, was declared the winner.

Although Tom Linton was nominally the victor of the series, it was an unsatisfactory conclusion to this long-awaited match. The antagonism between the one-time friends continued, although some commentators were of the opinion that the rift between the two was manufactured by their manager, Shafer, in a bid to arouse public interest and ensure good gate returns when they met. It was a hard, money-orientated business they were engaged in, so if this was the case, it should come as no surprise. Whatever the result of the race series, the public had been entertained, and both riders and their manager received ample financial reward for their efforts.

During the 1897 season, a new phenomenon had emerged onto the American cycle racing scene in the form of Marshall

Walter "Major" Taylor. He was born in Indianapolis, a city not far from the southern state of Kentucky. If he had been white, he would have been hailed as an American hero. But he was black, and his grandparents had been slaves. Despite having to endure extreme racial discrimination, he had fought his way to the top of his profession, and in 1898 became a member of a new racing organization, the American Cycle Racing Association, whose members included riders such as Fred Titus, Edouard Taylore, and Jimmy Michael. The group was set up as a direct challenge to the ruling body, the League of American Wheelmen, who had banned Negro membership. The public, at least in the northern states, however, wanted to see the best men matched against each other, irrespective of skin color.

In 1898 Major Taylor and Jimmy Michael were considered the best track racers in the world, so at the end of August they met in a special paced match at Manhattan Beach track in a contest of three one-mile races from a standing start. Jimmy easily won the first race, as Taylor's pacing machine broke down, but in the next two races, Jimmy was so far behind that he quit on the last lap, and for the first time in his career was hissed by the spectators. Taylors' riding not only gave him a new world record, but established him as a new star.

It was clear that Jimmy was better suited to middle-distance racing, and in September the two riders met again at the same venue, this time in a twenty-mile match, in front of some 5,000 spectators. Taylor could not match the killing pace set by Jimmy from the start, and despite several brave attempts, could not get anywhere near him, and as the distance ran out, he finished over two laps behind. The two matches showed where each men's talents lay. Both enjoyed a good pay day, and the public were satisfied.

During this period, Jimmy developed a friendship with a man who was to have a major influence on his life—and even his death. Jean Gougoltz was Swiss by birth, and French by adoption, a racing cyclist of some distinction on both road and track. He had won the Swiss championship at one km and the

French championship at two km in 1895. Through his exploits, he became known as the "Unpaced King of France." He later became an expert pacer, much in demand by top riders, and it was by this connection that he came to the notice of Jimmy Michael.

Gougoltz was a good companion, likeable and easygoing, but his weakness was an addiction to alcohol. When sober, he was delightful company, but when under the influence of drink he became abusive and violent. During one track meet, when he was disqualified for a misdemeanor during a race, he left the track, had several drinks, then returned and chased the promoter all over the velodrome with a knife.

As their friendship deepened, Jimmy, who had been a teetotaller most of his life, began to drink. Finding it gave a temporary relief from his problems, he became a regular drinker. This led to deterioration in his physical condition, and unless he changed his ways, would be on an inevitable slide to ruin. His manager, Dave Shafer, could see the way he was heading, so he put him into the hands of George S. McLeish, an experienced trainer who got him into condition and saved the day with wins over Chase, McDuffe, Starbuck, Titus, Taylore, and Lesna.

Fig. 6.8. Rising American star Major Taylor, who easily beat Jimmy Michael in their 1898 short-distance encounter, was no match for Michael over longer distances.

When the outdoor season came to a close in November, Jimmy and his new friend Gougoltz sailed from New York bound for Europe on an extended holiday. They would visit friends in Paris and Jimmy's family in Aberaman. Talking to reporters on the dock, Jimmy remarked that "he was disenchanted with cycle racing and in the New Year could possibly return to horse racing."

The "holiday" extended into 1899, and when in Paris, Jimmy contacted his equine friends, and secured rides on some of the best horses. However, for the second time he failed to make the grade as a jockey, his only success being a third place. He finally realized that his dream of escape was never going to be realized, and with most of his money now gone, he had no alternative but to return to the thing he did best—bicycle racing. Reluctantly, he made contact with his former cycle racing colleagues in the city and spent time getting into condition behind the motor tandems at the Parc des Princes velodrome.

On his return to America early the following year, he discovered that more of his money had disappeared due to fraud. It appears that he had paid $2,000 to a J. M. Murphy to purchase four race horses. However, the horses were never delivered, and it turned out that Murphy was only a part-owner of the horses and had no right to sell them. The affair, although taken to court, was never settled satisfactorily, while Jimmy lost his money. His

Left: Fig. 6.9. Jean Gougoltz, of Switzerland, was Jimmy Michael's constant companion and drinking-buddy in his later years.

venture into the sport of kings had been extremely expensive, and he realized too late that there were at least as many cheats and shysters operating in the horse-racing world as in cycle racing.

His decision to return to cycle racing proved more difficult than expected, as he found that his former manager, Dave Shafer, was unwilling to re-engage him, claiming that Jimmy's unreliability and lack of commitment made him unmanageable. Undeterred, he found a new manager in J. C. Kennedy, who was soon contacting promoters and arranging races. Jimmy's first ride was an exhibition ten-mile ride at the Buttonwood track in New Bedford, Massachusetts. It was billed, optimistically, as a world record attempt. Some 2,000 spectators paid their money to see if Jimmy Michael still possessed the magic that had made him a star.

He was paced by a motor-assisted tandem manned by an experienced crew. He went well, and seemed almost certain to break the record, then just before the distance ran out, he broke a crank and the attempt was abandoned. It was a gutsy performance; the spectators saw that he had done his best and went home happy.

The rest of the year was taken up fulfilling engagements throughout the country, but with only moderate success, and for the first time in an illustrious career, he failed to honor pledges to promoters to ride their events. He became so unreliable that he was reported to the National Cycling Association, who suspended him pending guarantees of future commitment. Eventually a compromise was reached that allowed him to continue racing.

Jimmy spent the early months of 1901 training and getting into shape, and by the spring he felt that he was ready to take on all comers. His first contest was in May, when he met Watson Coleman in a twenty-five mile exhibition ride at the Coliseum track in New York, which he won in a respectable time. The following month he traveled to Philadelphia and Boston to compete in two thirty-mile events, but was soundly beaten in both.

Early in July, Jimmy was back at the Manhattan Beach track in New York, where over 5,000 spectators gathered to watch local hero Harry Elkes and the emerging young hopeful Bobby Walthour being challenged by Jimmy in a one-hour motor-paced race. Jimmy was not in form, and despite frequently changing pacemakers, he struggled to take third place.

A week later, at the same venue, this time in a forty-mile race against Elkes and John Nelson, he showed that he was coming back into form by taking a well-deserved second place to Elkes. Later in the year, at Madison Square Garden, Jimmy soundly beat Bobby Walthour over three and five miles. This time he rode in a style reminiscent of his days of complete dominance over the best riders in the world. Racing continued into 1902, with a January meeting at the indoor track at the Second Regiment Armoury in Philadelphia. This time four riders competed in two five-mile motor-paced events, the riders being Jimmy Michael, Archie McEachern, Howard Freeman, and Jimmy's inseparable friend Jean Gougoltz. The result itself was not worthy of note, but during the evening Jimmy announced, "This will be my last meeting in America for some time, as I am leaving for Europe to ride some races there and will also ride a few horses."

Jimmy's return to European racing was initially successful, for at a meeting at the Buffalo track in Paris he easily beat Dangla and Anzani, and later at the same venue came fifth in the championship of France over 100 km, beating Jacquelin in convincing fashion. The remaining months of the year were spent cris-crossing Europe to compete in races and earn some money to replenish his bank balance, which had been so sadly depleted by his horse-racing exploits. 1903 was not a good year, for although still racing with some success, he was drinking heavily in the company of Jean Gougoltz.

On the 24th April he was at the Friedenau track in Berlin training behind a motor-pacer, when in a moment of lost concentration, he crashed. He lay unconscious, could not be revived, so was removed to a nearby hospital. The diagnosis was a fractured skull and multiple cuts and bruises. The doctors advised complete rest and a long stay in hospital for treatment. After a few days of inactivity, Jimmy felt better, and despite suffering from acute headaches, discharged himself. After a few days, he resumed racing, numbing the continuous headaches with large doses of alcohol.

In an article in *Cycling*, Victor Breyer, the journalist, promoter, and old friend, tells the story of Jimmy's slide into alcoholism:

> Being then in charge of programmes at the old Buffalo velodrome in Neuilly, I yielded to his [Jimmy Michael's] plan in agreeing to give him a last chance. This weakness I had cause to regret, for at the time appointed for the race he failed to turn up. After a wait, during which the public grew impatient, Gougoltz, who was to pace him and happened perchance to be in a normal state, volunteered to take me to a place where he felt sure to find his friend. Accordingly we drove in haste to a public-house near the Arc de Triomphe. There we found Michael sunk in an armchair close to the bar, visibly intoxicated. After some wrangling, Gougoltz prevailed on his pal to come to the track and fulfil his engagement
>
> An hour or so late, the race duly started with the Welsh boy among the competitors. What happened is easy to understand. The hitherto invincible "prodigy," losing lap after lap, finished a dab last, and left the track among hoots and hisses from that same

Right: Fig. 6.11. Jimmy Michael, resting on his cot at the Friedenau race track in Berlin, shortly before a serious crash caused severe brain injury, from which he would never recover.

crowd which had so often carried him back to his dressing room shoulder-high.

This was probably his last appearance on a track in Paris, as promoters were reluctant to book him, and it looked as though he had reached the end of his career. But no, a few weeks later he was back, racing in Antwerp, and in such good form that he beat Leander, Simar, Bouhours, Walthour, and Tom Linton. During the meeting, he set a new hour record behind a pacing motor without windshield, of 77.6 km.

Despite frequent bouts of drinking, 1904 was his best year since his accident in Germany, and he held form so well that promoters of the six-day races at Madison Square Garden offered him a contract to ride exhibition races during the main event, which he gladly signed up for.

So, on the 18th November, Jimmy and Gougoltz boarded the French liner Savoie bound for New York. With little else to do but wine and dine during the seven-day voyage, the two companions took full advantage of the cheap booze available to indulge in what had become their favorite pastime—drinking.

In the early hours of the 21st November, just twelve days after his twenty-ninth birthday, Jimmy got so hopelessly drunk

Left: Fig. 6.12. Post card sent from aboard the ocean liner Savoie, on which Jimmy Michael died in 1904.

in the bar that in the early hours of the morning, when everyone else had left, the barman had to carry him to his cabin. Later, when the steward attended to his cabin, he found Jimmy unconscious in his bunk, and was unable to wake him. The captain was informed and he called the ship's doctor, who pronounced him dead.

The death certificate stated that he had died from a brain convolution caused by Delirium Tremens (DT). DT can affect people after a period of heavy drinking, or people who have a history of regular drinking with periods of abstinence. It can also be triggered by a single head injury or a series of head injuries over a period of time. Jimmy Michael certainly qualified on both counts: he had become a heavy drinker, and during his years of competition, he was subjected to many falls while racing and training, and sustained a number of severe head injuries.

It was customary when people died on a boat for the captain to perform a burial service at sea, but Jean Gougoltz insisted that the body should continue to New York, so that internment could be in the country he had made his home. When the Savoie docked in the harbor, Jimmy's body was taken to Green Wood Cemetery in Brooklyn where he was laid to rest in an unmarked grave on the 29th November in the presence of a number of his

Right: Fig. 6.13. The 1949 reburial of Jimmy Michael's remains. Charles "Mile-a-Minute" Murphy is in the wheelchair; Frank Schwinn on the left.

racing friends and colleagues, who also met the cost of the funeral.

It was an ignominious departure for a man who had been hailed as a star and hero by thousands of people in Europe and America. Although public interest in paced racing in America faded soon after Jimmy's death, he was not forgotten by his former fans. On the 16th June 1922, a special one-hour motor-paced race was held in his honor at the New York velodrome and named the Prix Jimmy Michael.

His grave was never visited by his family and lay unattended for forty-five years, until the efforts of a group of racing old-timers who called themselves "The Bicycle Racing Stars of the 19th Century" began a search for the grave. It was finally located by Charles "Mile-a-Minute" Murphy, and the group decided that a headstone should be erected over the grave. The cost of the head stone, the bronze tablet, and their perpetual care was met by Frank W. Schwinn, whose father Ignaz had sponsored Jimmy when he first came to America.

The rededication ceremony took place at the cemetery on Sunday 12th June 1949. Among those in attendance were old racers Frank Kramer, Eddie McDuffe, Reggie McNamara, and Charles Murphy, who was by then wheelchair-bound. Jimmy's Welsh roots were not forgotten, as three members of the St. David's Society were in attendance. One of them had seen Jimmy race as a boy at Ponypridd in South Wales. Sadly, no member of the Michael family was present.

Chapter 7.

Choppy's Other Riders

CHOPPY WARBURTON often boasted, "I've only coached four riders, and three of them are now world champions." The riders he referred to were Arthur and Tom Linton, Jimmy Michael, and Amelie Le Gall—three Welshmen and a French woman. It was a boast to be proud of, but not quite true. During the seven years in which he coached cyclists, he maintained a stable of some thirty riders, mostly experienced, successful professionals, who earned a good living for themselves and Warburton.

Right: Fig. 7.1. Choppy with women's world champion Lisette Marton, whose real name was Amelie le Gall, of France, one of several women racers he trained and managed.

It is difficult to establish with certainty what riders, other than the Linton brothers and Jimmy Michael, were under the direct control of Warburton, as many rode for the Gladiator/Simpson team, either for a short period or a single event. The following riders are known to have a direct association with the trainer, but there must have been many more.

Constant Huret, the French champion, rode for Gladiator/Simpson from time to time, and was a close friend of the Lintons. Although he trained independently, he must have been influenced by Warburton's methods. After a glittering amateur career, Huret turned professional in 1895, and was immediately competing against Warburton's men on the Parisian tracks. Ironically, his career came to an abrupt end as a result of an accident involving Jimmy Michael. On the 4th September 1902, while taking part in a race at the Parc des Princes, Michael's tire burst, causing both riders to crash, and during the resulting entanglement, one of Michael's pedals dug deep into Huret's left leg. The injury was so severe that he was unable to ever ride competitively again.

Amelie le Gall was a sturdy Breton girl, better known in the cycle racing world by her sobriquet Lisette Marton, or more often simply Lisette. Warburton claimed that he discovered her tending sheep in the countryside near her home. How she got from this bucolic setting to the cut-and-thrust of cycle racing is unclear. Perhaps the story was just another example of Warburton's creative thinking, as he was a firm believer in the saying "never let the truth get in the way of a good story." Under his tutelage, she trained with the men, and as a result was considered unbeatable in matched sprinting against other women. She became part of the highly successful Gladiator/Simpson team, and went on to enjoy a successful racing career, winning the French version of the Woman's World Championship in Paris in 1896.

Under the imaginative management of Warburton, she partnered with Jimmy Michael in a mixed tandem race at Olympia, and later in a similar event with the French rider Jacquelin at the

Vélodrome d'Hiver. At the Islington Aquarium, Warburton matched her against Albert Champion. The result of that race is unknown, but it resulted in Champion being banned by the NCU, because their rules forbade mixed-sex racing. She later won several six-day races in London and Paris. On retiring from cycle racing, she married, moved to South America, and with her husband settled on a sheep-rearing ranch, and thus presumably back to her roots, if we can believe Choppy's story.

It is not known if the talented Scottish-born Mrs. Clara Grace was part of the Warburton menage, but she was certainly sponsored at one time by the Gladiator and Simpson companies, so it is likely she received some tuition from him. Clara was a highly successful amateur road and track rider, who turned professional in 1895. The following year she won the English National Championship on the road, broke records at 50 and 100 miles, shattered the London to Coventry and London to Brighton road

Above: Fig. 7.2. Hélène Dutrieux, shown here, also rode a Gladiator machine with Simpson Lever chain. She later gained world fame as an aviator.

Right: Fig. 7.3. Lisette, also on a Gladiator bicycle with Simpson Lever chain.

records, as well as winning many other races on the road and the track. She partnered with Charley Barden in the mixed tandem race at Olympia, competing successfully against Lisette and Jimmy Michael. The house at Wood Green where Warburton was lodging when he died in 1897 was owned by a Mr. Grace, possibly her father-in-law or husband. Whatever the relationship, it was a house frequented by cyclists, and well known to Warburton.

One of the last riders Warburton coached was Edouard Denieport. He was born in 1875 at Blida, Algeria, where his father was an officer commanding a garrison. Edouard was a shy, modest young man, but strong-willed and passionate about the things he took seriously. When the family moved to Paris, he enrolled as a student at the École Supérieure d'Électricité (Electrical Engineering School), and then onto the École Polytechnique (Engineering College) where he was one of their top students.

While still at college, he became interested in cycling, the latest craze among the upper classes. He discovered that with little training he could go faster than his friends, liked the sensation of speed, and took up racing. This caused much embarrassment to his bourgeois family, as racing cyclists were seen as rough boys from the working classes and should not mix with their betters. To his credit, class differences meant little to Edouard, and he would not be deterred from taking part in the sport, but did agree to change his name from Denieport to Nieuport, so that family and friends would not recognize his name when his racing exploits were reported in the newspapers.

He trained hard, enjoyed improved health and, although not as robust as his fellow competitors, nevertheless developed into a strong and determined sprinter. He enjoyed many victories, but his best performance was to win the Zimmerman Prize at the Seine Vélodrome in 1894. He was paced by sets of triplets and put so much effort into winning that he collapsed at the finish and had to be taken to hospital.

The following year was not as successful, as study restricted the time available for training. He nevertheless won ten handicap races on the Parisian tracks. By this time he was deeply involved in a subject that was to dominate his later life, and indeed was responsible for his death—aerodynamics. Not having the means to finance a laboratory and wind-tunnel to study the principles of aerodynamics, he devised the novel idea of using his body and a bicycle to carry out experiments.

His attention to detail for these tests was quite extraordinary. After looking at all the bicycles on the market, he chose a path racer made by the British Rudge-Whitworth company, as it had smooth contours and minimal wheel clearances. He had noticed that his fellow competitors invariably wore racing kit made of wool that had often become baggy through frequent use. He felt that this was an area where aerodynamic properties could be improved, so his custom-made racing strip was tailored in smooth material and skin-tight, so as to offer less air resistance when travelling at speed.

Right: 7.4. After his cycling career, Eduard Denieport, who took on the last name Nieuport, went on to become an aviation engineer. His Nieuport fighter planes were extensively used by the French military during World War I.

145

It was during this time that he sought the advice of a man he considered the best trainer in the world, Choppy Warburton. Choppy was so impressed by the young man's enthusiasm and dedication that he undertook to coach him. Surprisingly the young Frenchman from a good family enjoyed a good relationship with the rough old trainer from Lancashire. Perhaps they both recognized and respected each other's talents and were not constrained by their class differences. Unfortunately Warburton was destined to die the following year, so their association was short-lived. By coincidence Nieuport was in London that December when Warburton died, so was able to pay his respects to the family and attend the funeral service in person.

Nieuport continued racing after the death of his tutor, and in 1898 took third place in the French championships. Even when he retired from racing he still went to the tracks as a spectator and was very impressed by the performances of Major Taylor, the black American, when he came to Paris to compete against the French champion Edmond Jacquelin.

He went on to establish himself as one of the foremost aviation engineers in the world. It was when he was piloting an

Left: Fig. 7.6. Another one of Choppy's riders was Constant Huret, whose family became know for the development of derailleur gearing (above).

Facing page: Fig. 7.7. A. E. "Jenny" Walters, behind a motor-pace. Later he would improve the design of the bikes used for this discipline.

aircraft to Verdun on the 10th September 1911 that he crashed on landing and died of his injuries. For services to aviation he was posthumously awarded the Cross of the Legion of Honor.

Albert Edward "Jenny" Walters was born in London in 1870, and after leaving school enjoyed early success in cycle racing. He was invited to join the famous Polytechnic Cycling Club, where he built a reputation as a dependable long-distance track rider. After taking out a professional license, he made his way to Paris in 1896 to join Choppy Warburton and the Gladiator team

After Choppy's death, he was retained by the Gladiator team and continued using their standard track machines for paced racing. However, he became increasingly aware that the bicycles were unstable at the higher speeds being obtained since electric and motor- assisted tandems had been introduced. Having a mechanical turn of mind, "Jenny" put his ideas down on paper and approached Frank Fenton, the general manager of Gladiator, with his suggestions. Fenton immediately saw possibilities in the design, and gave him a note to the works manager instructing him to build a bicycle to Walter's design.

The basic idea was to shorten the wheelbase by decreasing the gaps between the frame and the wheels, raising the bottom bracket, and fitting a twenty-four inch wheel into straight front forks, which increased the bike's forward stability. These amendments also enabled the rider to get closer to the pacer, thus receiving more shelter as well as greater stability. Gearing

on conventional bicycles used for pacing was between 98 and 110 inches, but on these new machines gearing could be stepped up to 116 inches, making it possible to increase speed using the same pedaling rate. Bicycles used for pacing were built to the new design and issued to all the Gladiator riders, who were soon riding them to success.

Walters' best year was 1899, when he took second place in the European Stayer Championship and won the prestigious 24 hour Bol d'Or race behind an electric-powered tandem at the Parc des Princes track in Paris. He did not have a long career, and died in London in 1956.

Albert Champion was born in Paris in 1878. He took up cycle racing at an early age, turned professional in 1896, and joined Choppy Warburton at the same time as "Jenny" Walters, both specializing in paced track racing. Much to everyone's surprise, he entered the Paris–Roubaix road race in 1899. By that time the human pacing machines used previously had been replaced by motor-powered pacers, and Albert Champion, having had considerable experience behind the motors, thought this would give him an advantage. But he had not made allowances for the atrocious road conditions and the infamous cobbles. Just the same, despite being slowed by hunger, and riding the cobbles at

Left: Fig. 7.8. Albert Champion was another one of Choppy's riders. When Choppy organized a race for Champion and Lisette, he was banned by the NCU. After retirement he made his fortune with automotive spark plugs. He too died a tragic death, but it had nothing to do with Choppy, nor even with bicycle racing for that matter.

walking pace, he won with 23 minutes over second-placed Paul Bor.

Chasing the money, and it was said to escape conscription into the army, he went to America to race, where he competed against most of the top riders, including Jimmy Michael and Tom Linton. Although enjoying some success, and building a reputation as a strong rider, his main interest was in the newly emerging motor industry in America and the development of racing cars. In 1904 he returned to France to continue racing, and although he won the French motor-paced championship, his mind was on other things. Away from racing, he spent time developing his ideas on spark plugs and magnetos. Having perfected a design, he returned to America in 1905, and abandoned cycle racing to establish the Champion Spark Plug Company.

Manufacturing spark plugs under his name, he became a wealthy man, returned to France, where he divorced his wife to marry a much younger woman. After five years of marriage, suspecting his wife of infidelity, Champion followed her to a

Right: Fig. 7.5. Choppy Warburton "launching" Eros, another one of his riders, who went only by that single name.

149

Parisian night club on October 27th 1927, where she had arranged a rendezvous with her lover, one Charles Brazelle. An angry confrontation ensued, in which Champion received a severe beating that left him barely able to walk, and he died in his hotel room a few hours later.

Chapter 8.

Other Trainers and Their Charges

THERE WERE many managers and trainers of racing cyclists in England and America during the 1890s, but few, if any, had the ability and charisma of Choppy Warburton. His influence was such that he was respected by riders, and feared by the racing authorities, who felt he had too much control over the sport, and continually conspired against him in an attempt to restrict his influence. Aided by the actions of his top riders, they succeeded in banning his activities in the U.K. His top rider, Jimmy Michael was "poached" by Tom Eck and taken to America, introduced into the racing circuits there, and made a lot of money.

Tom Eck was an American contemporary of Warburton, although fourteen years his junior. He was not only a nationally respected trainer and manager, but a showman in the Barnum and Bailey sense. He would seize every opportunity, however bizarre, to make money.

Thomas W. Eck, known as "Beauty," claimed he was born an Englishman. However, the 1895 census records for Hennepin, Minneapolis, USA, which shows him living at 2802, 2nd Street, with his wife Jennie and daughter Jane, gives his birthplace as Canada. His early life and education is unknown, although as a young man he had been an all-round sportsman. He had in turn been jockey, horse trainer, lacrosse player, and skater of some renown. The first time his name appears in a newspaper was when he arrived in the U.S. in 1880 as a high-wheel racer, contracted to ride for Gormully & Jeffrey, makers of the famous Rambler bicycles. The biography of American champion Stillman G. Whittaker, has this to say about Tom Eck:

> ... he landed in St Louis with his wife Louise Armaindo, the great women racer, John S. "Jack" Prince and a few others, looking for opportunities to promote bicycle racing. Eck was an ex-Canadian champion high wheel racer who had settled in Minneapolis, and was beginning his career as manager and promoter extra-ordinaire...
>
> He brought him [Whittaker] to his home town of Minneapolis for a huge bicycling and roller-skating extravaganza. At that time, Eck was working toward bringing the six-day bicycle races, which had been so popular in England, to America. This was the last test event before he finally promoted America's first all-bicycle six-day race, held two weeks later at this same venue. He built an eight-laps-to-the-mile, slightly banked, bicycle track around the skating track at the Washington Roller Rink. Commencing on George Washington's birthday, it was a week-long fest alternating bicycle racing with skating races.

Whittaker was the featured cyclist in what was billed as St. Louis vs. Minneapolis. Ever the showman, Eck met him [Whittaker] at the railway depot with a brass band and a contingent of local wheelmen.

Eck was in it for the money as much as the sport. The spring of 1888 saw the Gormully & Jeffrey team in Philadelphia for some last-minute racing before it embarked for England. The six-day bicycle racing which Eck had initiated was sweeping the nation. Eck had the entire troupe present: Whittaker, Hollingsworth, McDowell, Rhodes, Ashinger, Neilson, Crocker, Knapp, Dingley, his wife Louise Armaindo, and himself.

Louise Armaindo was a remarkable women. She was born Louise Brisbois in St. Ann, Quebec, Canada, in 1861. She showed remarkable strength and athletic ability from an early age. By her early twenties, she stood five feet two inches tall and weighed one hundred and twenty-two pounds. With her dark curly hair, black eyes, and a full, busty figure, she was much admired at the time, so was popular with the male spectators. As the niece of Joe Muffaro, a well-known French strong-man who appeared in vaudeville shows, she was able to arrange an introduction to a theater impresario, and was soon appearing in halls throughout North America, performing amazing feats of strength. It is said she could lift 760 pounds above her head, and hold dumbbell weighing 105 pounds at arm's length.

She demonstrated her athletic ability by running twenty miles non-stop and walking for twenty-four hours without a break at Madison Square Garden, New York. Her feats on the high-wheel bicycle were no less spectacular. Mounted on a nickel-plated Royal Mail machine, she rode 760 miles in six days at the Armory in Washington. At the Old Mechanics pavilion in

Above and right: Figs. 8.1 and 8.2. Tom Eck in his younger days, when he was known as "Beauty," and in later years (right).

San Francisco, partnering with John Prince, she rode a special six-day race, humans against horses. They each rode their high bicycles for alternate hours against Charles Anderson riding horses, who changed mounts after each mile. Armaindo and Prince rode a total of 1,076 miles, beating Anderson by five miles.

At Bismarck, she competed in a five-mile cycle race against her husband for a purse of $300, which she won. According to the *Leavenworth Times* of September 1883, "…the race would not have attracted any notice at all, had it not been for the scanty attire worn by Miss Armaindo."

Many sections of society still considered that women who took part in cycle races were brazen, immoral, and little more than burlesque entertainers, and supported the myth of female frailty in sport. Eck though, fully supported female emancipation in sport, and seized every opportunity to promote his bevy of cycling beauties. In July 1885 he booked Washington Park in Brooklyn for three days to stage a man versus horse race. The trio of Armaindo, Prince, and Eck mounted on high-wheel bicycles would race every afternoon against a Mexican cowboy named M. Spencer riding a horse. The result of the races was immaterial—the important thing was that it was reported in all the newspapers. It was another publicity coup, as the event successfully raised the trio's profile, resulting in more bookings and greater earnings.

The following year, Eck was reported in the January issue of *Sporting Life* to have beaten the national quarter-mile tricycle record on the Springfield track. In 1889, Eck assembled a troupe of female riders he called "The Pittsburgh Girls" to compete in a series of six-day races in all the principal cities of Europe. The four American girls, Lottie Stanley, Jesse Woods, Lilly Williams, and May Allen, were all competent high-wheel riders, and were more than capable of handling the rough-and-tumble of European racing. The highlight of their trip was competing in a special six-day race in Paris, where they rode twelve hours a day against a team of cowboys mounted on horses in Buffalo Bill's Wild West Show.

How Louise Armaindo and Tom Eck first met is unknown, but when she retired from cycle racing in 1911, and was asked which of her strong-women feats she regarded as her best she replied, "Having the strength to know when to appear weak when the right man asked for my hand." Was that man Tom Eck? No official record of Eck's marriage to Louise Armaindo can be found, so perhaps they were, to use the modern phase, partners.

Press reports from the period always refer to the couple as man and wife. To add to the mystery, a new woman appeared in his life. In *An American Cycling Odyssey*, written by Kevin J. Hayes, the section on John S. Prince states: "Prince also had an excellent reputation for his hospitality. Later that summer he and his wife would open their home on 15th Street to Tom Eck and Jenny Carlisle, the Canadian cycling champion and his bride-to-be, for their wedding." No evidence of a divorce from Armaindo can be found, making the mention of his "bride-to-be" rather confusing. Eck's marital affairs were never simple, as two articles published in the *New York Times* in 1888 show. It is worthwhile quoting the articles in full, as they give an insight into the complex character of Eck:

ROMANCE QUICKLY SPOILED
A BRIDE AT SIXTEEN A YEAR AGO NOW SEEKING DIVORCE.
Minneapolis – Just a year ago last Friday pretty little Jennie Carlisle,

Right: Fig. 8.3. Tom Eck's presumed wife, Louise Armaindo, seen from the back, flexing her mighty muscles.

155

the daughter, 16 years old, of a Minneapolis business man, eloped with "Beauty" Eck, a professional bicyclist, who is perhaps better known in Minneapolis than any other sporting man who ever made his headquarters here. This afternoon Mrs. T. Eck filed a complaint in a divorce suit against Thomas W. Eck alleging infidelity and cruelty. There is a little romance and a great deal of hard reality compressed into a year between the elopement and the divorce suit, if Mrs. Eck's story is true. The fascinating bicyclist was a great friend of Miss Carlisle's brother Steve, a little more than a year ago, and Steve Carlisle backed Eck in one or two races, Eck was, very naturally, often at the Carlisle residence, and made the most of his opportunities to ingratiate himself in the affections of Miss Jennie, who was then a schoolgirl and in whose eyes the handsome "sport" easily magnified himself into a hero.

Eck diverted suspicion by making himself very agreeable to an elder sister. One day Miss Jennie gave it out that she was going to visit a friend and would be gone all day. She went straight to "Beauty" and he and the little miss took the first train for Omaha, where they were married. The affair created something of a sensation at the time. Miss Carlisle's family were very indignant, but they finally forgave the two and they came to Minneapolis to live. They afterward went to Philadelphia, where they lived for three months, and where it is claimed, Eck treated his wife with great brutality, once threatening to shoot her. Mrs. Eck came home to her parents about April last, and soon after that time Eck went to Europe, where he is in charge of the American team of bicyclists.

A further report on the affair appeared in *The New York Times* on the 6th October 1888:

RUNNING OFF WITH HIS WIFE
HOW TOM ECK STOPPED SOME DIVORCE PROCEEDINGS
St. Paul, Minneapolis, October 5 – Tom Eck, the bicyclist, is as renowned in love as he is on his machine. It was only a few moons ago when the public was treated to the full details of his romantic courtship and final clandestine marriage with a young

lady of Minneapolis, Miss Jennie Carlisle, living with her parents at Second Street and Twenty-eighth Avenue, North. The course of true love was not all that smooth. A short time after the marriage Eck left Minneapolis for his favourite haunts at Chicago and other cities further East, and the gossips had it that he had already tired of his young wife. At any rate, she began proceedings for a divorce two months ago, alleging desertion. Last Sunday Eck appeared in Minneapolis again, supposedly to take some action in regard to the divorce. He kept pretty quiet all the week until yesterday, when he came down, like Lochinvar from the West, and stopped proceedings by carrying off his wife to parts unknown. Her parents, with whom she was living, affirm that it was done forcibly, but that belief is not shared by others of the family. It is said that they accidentally met on Nicollet Avenue, and he hurried her into a hack, which was driven to the Union Station, whence they were whisked off behind the iron horse.

The missing wife's father reported the case at Police Headquarters, and requested that they capture Eck if possible, as he believed that his daughter had not accompanied him of her own free will. The police at St. Paul were accordingly put on the alert, but up to a late hour nothing had been heard from them. The brother of Mrs. Eck expressed himself as not at all surprised at the turn in affairs. It was not her doings, he said, that divorce proceedings were begun, and in his opinion she loved Eck well enough to run away with him any day in the week. He took no stock in the belief that she was not a party to the runaway. It is stated that the parents have never taken kindly to Eck, and that it was at their insistence that the action for divorce was begun. However it may be, the young couple are together, and the probabilities are that the divorce will never come to trial.

If the date of Eck's and Carlisle's marriage is correct, then why was Eck still racing in partnership with Armaindo a year later? Whatever happened during that period was sorted out, and the couple stayed together for the remainder of their natural lives. The episode gives an indication of how well-known Eck was in

America: To have a domestic dispute that happened in a state in the centre of the country reported by a major newspaper on the east coast, more than a thousand miles away, was fame indeed. The incident also shows how popular racing on high-wheelers was in America, and how interested the public were in the lives of the star riders. This interest turned to adoration some ten years later, when the invention of the pneumatic tire and the introduction of multi-rider pacing machines dramatically increased racing speeds and the danger.

By this time, Eck had retired from racing, and had taken on the mantle of trainer, manager, and promoter extraordinaire. He continued to promote bicycle races, and indeed anything spectacular to make money. By 1894 he controlled a stable of some forty riders of various abilities. His training methods were in many ways similar to those of Choppy Warburton. He was a man of striking appearance, with a walrus moustache and prematurely white hair, resulting in him being known as "The Silver Haired Veteran." Clever and capable, with all the tricks of the trade at his finger tips, he knew everyone and everyone knew him. He was a disciplinarian, expecting complete and unquestioned obedience from his riders, both in training and racing, he would think nothing of locking unruly riders in their hotel bedrooms when they wanted to hit the town during racing trips away from home.

His training methods were not revolutionary, but based on a sensible diet, plenty of rest, sleep, and quality mileage. He wrote a book on training called *Points on Training for Wheelmen*. The book was published by E. C. Stearns in 1895, but to date no surviving copy has been found. Fortunately his views on the subject were reported in the *New York Times* on the 14th January 1894, under the title "How to Train for a Cycle Race":

> ... The man who contemplates racing next year should begin
> about the first of April to prepare himself, by taking several doses
> of physic every other day, and during that time eat plenty of light
> food, such as oatmeal, rice pudding, bread and milk, soft-boiled

eggs, and food of that nature. After that, with a rest of four days, begin light work on your wheel, say a spin of from three to five miles twice a day. I don't believe in long work at the start. After a week of this kind of work you can go 200 yards at a good sprint about once a day, and take spins of from three to five miles at a good fast clip, as you must now begin to work for your wind. And good sweats are essential. After two weeks of such work, a rider can begin to repeat in his work – that is to say, on Monday, after resting on Sunday, you go out and ride a trial of a quarter of a mile almost at top speed, then come in, take a good rub-down, and, after a rest of twenty minutes or half an hour, to and ride it over again at you best speed.

Note the time in each trial, and, in fact, in all your trials, time each one. Then you can see how you are improving, and if you are taking the right kind of work. As long as you improve, keep up the same work. If you don't improve, let up a day or two, and change onto longer and slower work for a week, and no speeding at all. Then do some more repeating. Never repeat over twice a week after you get so you can go a full half or mile. You must do the quarter-mile repeats first for a week, then the half-mile the next week. But make them in the afternoon, and in the mornings do stiff work for three to five miles. Never loaf around on the track, just after you work, but always come in while the perspiration is still on your body. Cover up well for a few minutes, then rub-down, one part of the body at a time, keeping the other parts covered. See there are no draughts in the training quarters, and prevent catching cold. One of the principal features in your training is to sweat. When you do not sweat, you are not right. This is a sure sign.

Racing men should eat plenty of vegetables and soft food, and not all beefsteak and mutton chops. I believe in steaks and chops, or meat of any description, except pork. Any kind of fruit a man likes is good – in fact, it is grass to a man. Another thing a man should look to is his sleep. Take two men of equal speed, and the one who will go to bed early and rest will win the race the following day. Sleep is very essential to a man's best speed. Nine to 9:30 PM is the time to be in bed, and rise at 7 AM, taking a good rub-down with the hands, and the same on retiring at night. Hand rubbing beats any kind of towel or instrument that can be used. Walking around is tiresome, and makes the muscles stiff and sore.

If a man would condition himself like a racehorse, he would be able to cover a mile much faster, and repeat his races oftener, and his muscles would not harden-up, as they do with so much walking around. Running is not beneficial to a cyclist, run as little as possible, in fact, do all your work on your wheel. It will not hurt a man to go out on the road for a five-mile ride whilst in training. It takes the monotony of the track off your mind. But when you go out on the road, remember you are not out for a scorch, you are out for a little recreation. Don't drink soda water on these rides; take a glass of good milk. A man can drink all he wants during training, and during the racing season, except on the day he races.

A man will make poor headway in his work unless he has every confidence in his trainer. A trainer cannot preach one thing to his man and then not act on it himself. The trainer must train like his man, as to habits, eating, sleeping. The trainer must know how to read men's dispositions and judge well their different nature. Nothing sounds so bad as to hear a man swearing in the dressing room, it lowers a man in the estimation of other riders and disgusts any visitors present. If you should beat a man during practice, don't boast about it in the dressing room, for others can do that for you. You should always have plenty of towels and liniment of your own and not have to borrow from others. The same goes for tools and oil. Never ask a racing man to let you try his wheel, he will not want to. Always have plenty of clean clothing for training, always look neat in training and racing, for you cannot tell when ladies may be present and nothing looks so nice as a well-dressed athlete.

It would appear, though, that Eck had some strange ideas on bicycle maintenance. In 1895 the *New York Times* reported:

The Tom Eck remedy for keeping the chain free from grit and dirt throughout the season is very simple. His idea, and he always uses it with [John S.] Johnson's wheels [bicycles], is to "take the chain from wheel and give it a good scrubbing with benzene [otherwise known as petroleum ether and highly inflammable] or some similar fluid. After the chain has been dried thoroughly, it is inserted in boiling tallow and allowed to remain for several minutes; then it is taken and dropped heavily on the floor to cleanse it. After being rubbed briskly, it is ready for plain bicycle oil, which should be rubbed well into every link. After that a drop or two of oil a month, will keep it in limber and perfect. It is a simple direction, and one that every rider can afford to consider."

By the 1890s, there were over a hundred cycle racing tracks in America. Many were little more than updated cinder tracks, but as the public interest in cycle racing grew, many timber and concrete banked tracks were constructed. More than 600 professional riders were competing on a nationally organized circuit. Eck was in his element, busy all the time, rushing from one meeting to another. At the end of a race it was not unusual for him to hop on a train to another city, fix up rides for his men with a promoter, barely have time for a cup of coffee before jumping on another train to another city.

He was making money, lots of it, and living the style to which he had become accustomed. He was always on the lookout for new riders. During a trip to England, he was told about a sensational young Welsh rider, diminutive, but as strong as an ox. Eck wanted him, but before committing himself, he needed to meet the rider in person. That's what brought him to the Catford track for the Chain Races on 6th June 1896, where Jimmy Michael would be riding.

Earlier that year, Ignaz Schwinn, maker of the famous Schwinn bicycles, had contracted the American star rider John S. Johnson to ride his machines. Eck was engaged to train Johnson, with the added responsibility of knocking into shape the riders that would drive the newly built Schwinn multi-manned pacing machines, as paced racing was just beginning to gain popularity in America. At that time, the best paced riders in the world were in Europe, so Eck put together a team of American riders, backed by Schwinn, called them The World Team, and sailed for Europe early in March. They raced in most of the major capital cities, arriving in London late in May to complete their tour.

Through his English contacts, Eck had been kept informed of Jimmy Michael's excellent racing performances. Arrangements were made for them to meet in London before what had already become known as the Chain Matches. They met in a discreet luxury hotel in Mayfair where Eck was staying, and over dinner Eck laid out his proposition to the Welshman to take him to America and introduce him into the lucrative racing circuit there. To Michael the sums of money talked about were way beyond his expectations. The only difficulty was his current contract with Warburton. The contract had been checked by lawyers and was watertight, and escape from it would be expensive. It was a cost Michael could not meet, and one that Eck was not willing to fund either, because Jimmy Michael had yet to prove his capabilities in the United States. There was a way out, Eck advised, if Michael was willing to take it: accuse Warburton of attempting to poison him.

Warburton's little black bottle and its mysterious contents was well known to all cycle racing aficionados, so it would be easy for Michael to feign a need for its recuperative powers, fall ill, and loudly declare that Warburton had poisoned him. Michael agreed to the ruse and suggested that the forthcoming Chain Matches, where he was due to compete, would present an ideal opportunity to act out the farce. The deception succeeded. Having fulfilled their contract obligations, Eck and his World Team left for America immediately after the races, followed by Jimmy Michael, who sailed for New York late in August.

After his arrival, Michael trained hard, and in a few weeks was racing fit. Early in September he appeared in an exhibition match against the American star rider Frank Starbuck. Later that month, Frank Fowler, a Chicago bicycle manufacturer, offered to back Starbuck in an hour race against Michael and deposited $500 at the track to bind the match. When Eck was asked to match the sum, he dramatically waived aloft a big roll of notes, loudly declaring "that to him, that amount of money was no problem," but to his embarrassment, when it was counted, it turned out to be some dollars short of the total. A heated debate ensued, resulting in both parties agreeing to meet the following day at the offices of *The Wheel* to pay the money and sign the contract. Presumably, the race did eventually take place.

Eck was annoyed at losing a talented, money-making machine such as Michael, but on the other hand he was relieved to be no longer tied to such a difficult character. Not to be outdone and lose the magic Michael name, early in 1898 he journeyed to Wales, signed up Michael's brother Willie, who was a good journeyman rider, and took him back to America, where he gave a good account of himself on the racing circuit. In 1903 Eck still had 35 to 40 riders under contract, including Lottie Brandon, the talented woman rider from Peterborough, Canada. She held every record from a quarter to 100 miles, and was the first women to ride a mile in less than two minutes.

Below: Fig. 8.4. Trained by Eck, the Schwinn pacing team was perhaps the strongest such team in America.

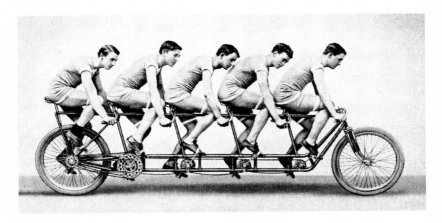

Eck carried on promoting cycling, and any other event that would show a profit. In Paris he operated a "Wall of Death," with two cyclists riding round-and-round, their ability to ride vertically without falling off astonishing the audience. He had plans to engineer a complete globe, so that the riders could loop the loop, but as the riders were unable to attain the speed required, and kept falling to the bottom of the globe, he abandoned the idea. He ended his days as a track- and-field trainer at the University of Chicago. He died in 1926 aged sixty-seven. His final resting place is unknown.

Perhaps the last word should go to Pridmore and Hurd, the authors of the book *Schwinn Bicycles*. Their description of Eck nicely sums up his complex character:

> ... he was a silver-haired, intense man, whose commitment to winning gained him more victories than it did friends. Indeed, there probably was room for gentlemen in the world of pro racing at this time; Tom Eck was not usually counted among them. Yet Eck understood better than most that respect in racing came not from good fellowship, but from winning races and setting records. As a result, his determination to succeed was obvious to all who knew him. He often glared at opponents before the start of a race in an attempt to unnerve them. He was not above pulling strings to keep top competition out of races... On other occasions, the trainer could become so frustrated that he physically attacked opponents.

Sam Mussabini, another famed trainer, had a tenuous link to Choppy Warburton in that he was once engaged to train the Dunlop pacing team after it had been soundly beaten by the Gladiator pacers. Scipio Africanus Mussabini was born in London to a middle-class family in 1867. As his exotic name implies, he was of Arab-Turkish-French ancestry. He received a good education, and although excelling in academic subjects, still found time to take an active part in athletics and, surprisingly, that most English of games, cricket. He was also an accomplished billiard player, fascinated by the technique and skill required to play the game competitively.

On completion of his formal education, he followed his father into journalism, an occupation he was involved in throughout his life. His early interest in athletics occupied much of his leisure time. He was inspired by activities of the sprinter Harry Hutchins and the middle-distance runner Walter George, a one-time opponent of Choppy Warburton. His approach to training was analytical, and he developed a system that was so successful that he became a professional sprinter.

Although moderately successful, he realized that he lacked the physical attributes to become a first-class athlete, so used his skills in coaching. He is the acknowledged creator of the saying "You cannot put in what God left out." His analytical approach to training placed him substantially ahead of his contemporaries. For

Above and right: Figs. 8.5 and 8.6. Sam Mussabini with the runner William Applegarth (left) at the 1912 Olympic Games, and as portrayed by Sir Ian Holm in the film Chariots of Fire (above). Mussabini also trained a number of cycling champions, including the Dunlop pacing team.

example, he was so inspired by the experiments of Edward Muybridge in photographing the action of athletes in motion, that in the early 1920s he bought a cine camera to record the movements of the men he was coaching to ensure their posture and stride patterns were correct for their physical type.

The development of professional cycle racing in the early 1890s attracted many coaches from the world of athletics. They were employed not only by the large bicycle and tire manufactures, but also by the committees of wealthy sports clubs. Sam was employed by one of the top clubs in the country, the Polytechnic in London. His first major success with the club was steering the Polytechnic Cycling Club rider Bert Harris to success in the first Professional Championship organized by the National Cyclists Union in 1896.

After the drubbing the Dunlop pacing team had received by the Gladiator's in the Chain Races, Sam was engaged by the Dunlop Tyre Company to coach the riders and improve the standard of their pacing. After several months of hard work, they emerged re-energized and were later acknowledged as the best pacing team in the world, with Sam's reputation as a coach further enhanced.

During the winter months, Sam used his journalistic skills to report on billiards for newspapers, and in 1897 he collaborated in writing a technical book on the game. He was also writing articles for a newly launched billiards journal, and in 1902 he was appointed assistant editor, later taking over as editor and proprietor. In 1904 he wrote a two-volume work on the technicalities of billiards that became the definitive work on the game. He became one of the top referees of the sport, travelling all over the country in charge of important tournaments.

In 1911 he coached several Polytechnic sprinters in preparation for the 1912 Olympic Games in Stockholm, some of them winning gold medals. His continued success with the club's athletes resulted in Sam being appointed their full-time official coach, a post he held until his death in 1927. His coaching methods were so successful that in the 1920 Antwerp Olympics his athlete Albert Hill won a gold medal in both the 800 and 1,500 meters, with Harry Edwards taking bronze in the 100 meter sprint. The performance of his athletes in the 1924 Paris Olympics are better known through being featured in the film "Chariots of Fire," in which Sam Mussabini, portrayed by the actor Sir Ian Holm, coached Harold Abrahams to a gold medal in the 100 meter sprint and a silver medal in the 4 X 100 meter relay. In five Olympic Games, spanning 21 years, the athletes coached by Sam were awarded an astonishing 11 medals.

Few cyclists know that Sam lived at 84 Burbage Road, London, from 1913 to his death in 1927. He chose to live there because the billiard room led into the garden and from there direct access into the grounds of Herne Hill Stadium. This enabled him to watch his beloved athletes and cyclists in action. The majority of the runners and riders had no idea who the little old man was who took such an interest in their training.

In 1988 it was decided to create an award to be called The Mussabini Medal for Coaching. Since inauguration, 48 people have received the award, including Sir Alf Ramsey and Sir Alex Ferguson for football, Ron Pickering for athletics, and Peter Keen and Simon Jones for cycling. Sam has also been nominated for a Blue Plaque to be erected at Herne Hill.

Although Sam Mussabini and Choppy Warburton were decades apart, they shared a common ambition: to be the best in their chosen profession. Warburton was a pioneer trainer, when the occupation was treated with suspicion and viewed almost as a black art. Mussabini, born twenty-two years after Warburton, was a new breed of trainer, using all available science and technology, but even he was ostracized by the athletic establishment for being a paid coach. Although attitudes toward trainers and coaches have changed considerably, athletic coaches are still not allowed in the track area and have to shout instructions to their charges from the stands. There is no evidence to show that the two men ever met, but they must have been aware of each other in the restricted field of athletics and cycle racing.

Bibliography and Sources

A. Books

Bartleet, H. W. *Bartleet's Bicycle Book*. London: Ed. J. Burrow & Co., 1931.

Jacobs, Barbara. *The Dick Kerr's Ladies*.

Perry, David B. *Bike Cult: The Ultimate Guide to Human-Powered Vehicles*. New York: Four Walls Eight Windows, 1995.

Pommier, Gérard. *Nieuport: A Biography of Edouard Nieuport*. Atglen (USA): Schiffer Publishing: 2007.

Pridmore, J. and J. Hurd. *Schwinn Bicycles*. Osceola (USA): Motorbooks International, 1996.

Ritchie, Andrew. *King of the Road: An Illustrated History of Cycling*. London: Willowood House / Berkeley: Ten Speed Press, 1975.

—. *Major Taylor: "The Fastest Bicycle Rider in the World."* San Francisco: Bicycle Books, 1988; Cycle Publishing, 2009.

—. *Quest for Speed: A History of Early Bicycle Racing, 1868–1903*. Published by the author, 2011.

Smith, Robert A. *A Social History of the Bicycle: Its Early Life and Times in America*. New York: American Heritage Press.

Swann, Dick. *The Life and Times of Charlie Barden*.

—. *Bert Harris of the Poly: A Cycling Legend*.

Taylor, Marshal W. "Major." *The Fastest Bicycle Rider in the World*. Worcester (USA): Wormley Publishing, 1928.

Watson, Richard O. *"Choppy" Warburton: Long-distance Runner and Trainer of Cycling Champions*. Privately published, 2010.

Woodland, Les. *The Crooked Path to Victory: Drugs and Cheating in Professional Bicycle Racing*. San Francisco: Cycle Publishing, 2003.

B. British Magazines and Newspapers

Cycling

The Times

The Hub

The Boneshaker

The Aberaman Times

Cycling World Illustrated

Sporting Cyclist

C. American Magazines and Newspapers

Sporting Life

The New York Times

The Cycle Age and Trade Review

Police Review

Daily Alta

Spalding's Official Bicycle Guide for 1898

American Bicyclist and Motorcyclist

D. Australian Magazines and Newspapers

Victoria Daily Colonist

E. Websites

Hundreds—too many to list.

F. Personal Sources

Richard O. Watson, for allowing the author unlimited access to his research on Choppy Warburton;

Ray Miller, librarian of the Veteran Cycle Club, who spent many hours in patient research;

Andrew Ritchie, for American sources;

Stuart Stanton, for Welsh sources;

Philip O'Donoghue, for German translations;

Scotford Lawrence, for French translations;

Lorne Shields, for information on Tom Eck;

Also the many, many, people who gave me tips on where to look for information;

Last and certainly not least, my wife Alma, for her patience and forbearance, for without her help this book would not have been written.

G. Illustration Sources

Cycle Publishing collection: 2.12, 2.13

Gronen & Lemke: Figs. 2.3, 2.4, 2.5, 2.7, 7.7

Tony Hadland: Fig. 6.3

Andrew Ritchie collection: 2.10, 6.8

Author's collection: all other images.

Index

A

Aberaman, 62, 68, 79, 88, 105, 116
Aberaman Cycling Club, 22, 71, 88, 108–109, 118
Aberaman Ladies Cycling Club, 118
Aberdare, 108
American Cycle Racing Association, 132
American Middle-Distance Championship, 102
Anfield Bicycle Club, 85
Applegarth, William, 165
Armaindo, 152–157
Arnold Schwinn & Co, 119
arsenic, 63

B

Bald, Eddie, 122
Barden, Charley, 40, 47, 49
"Beauty," as nickname for Tom Eck, 151
Bernard, Tristan, 45–46
betting, NCU position on, 41
Bicycle Racing Stars of the 19th Century, the, 140
Bloch, Stella, 32
Bol d'Or, 87, 148
Bonhours, 96, 104
Bor, Paul, 149
Bordeaux–Paris, 34, 83–87, 91, 95
    results, 86
Bougle, Louis ("L. B. Spoke"), 44, 47
Bouhours, 138
Brady, Bill, 129
Brandon, Lottie, 163
Breyer, Victor, 82–83, 110, 137
Buffalo Bill, (see Cody, William)
Buffalo Vélodrome, 32, 46
Butler, Tom, 122

C

caffeine, 63
Cardiff Horticultural Society Sports Day, 80
Carlisle, Jennie, 155–157
Carlisle, R. H. "Doc," 83, 85–87
Carr and Bank Mills, 11
Catford Cycling Club, 44, 88
Catford six-hour race, 112
Catford track, 44, 47–48, 50, 52, 87, 96
Chain Races, 37, 45–52, 50, 87, 96
Champion, Albert, 44, 56, 59, 97, 104, 143, 148, 150
    marital problems and death, 150
Charles River track, 99, 122
Charron, Fernand, 128
Chase, Arthur Adalbert, 40, 52, 82, 114, 123–125, 133
Chinn, H., 82
Choppy, origin of nickname, 10
class system, 7
coca, 64
Coca-Cola, introduced as patent medicine, 64
cocaine, 63–64
Cody, William, ("Buffalo Bill") 22–23, 74, 155
Coleman, Watson, 135
"Collier Boy," as nickname for Arthur Linton, 22
Cordang, Mathieu, 86
Crystal Palace, 98
Cuca Cocoa, 65
Cuca Cocoa Challenge Cup, 22, 64–65, 64 73
Cuca-Fluide, 64
Cyclists' Touring Club, 65
Cynon Valley, 68, 94
Cynon Valley Museum and Gallery, 94

D

Daisy Races, 40
Dance, S. F., 110
Denieport, Edouard (*see also* Nieuport), 144
Desgrange, Henri, 73
dietary regimes, 24
Dring, John, 44, 82
drug use in early sports, 67
drug use in early sports, 64ff
Dubois, Jules, 75–76, 112
Duckwork, John, 12
Dugdale-Astley, Sir John, "Sporting Barron," 18
Dunlop pacing team, 33, 48, 53, 94, 166
Dutrieux, Hélène, 143
Dwyer, Phil, 128

E

Eck, Thomas W., 52, 55, 97, 118–121, 127, 151–163
    at Chain Races, 52, 161
    and Jimmy Michael's contract with Warburton, 162
    and marital problems, 155–156
    and training methods, 158–160
    death of, 164
Edwards, Laurie, 58
eight-day race, 77–78
Elkes, Harry, 99, 102, 104–105, 136
Eros, 149

F

Fenton, Frank, 147
Finsbury Cycling Club, 38
Fischer
Fischer, Josef, 23, 34–35, 83–84
Fisherman's Arms, 14
fixing of races, 29

Freeman, Howard, 136

G

Gamage, Albert Walter, 38–41
    and women's racing, 40
Gamage Cycling and Athletic Club, 38–39
Garin, Maurice, 83–84
George, Walter, 165
Gladiator company, 31, 44, 52–53
    hostel, 44, 74, 81, 96, 111
    pacing team, 31, 52–53, 101, 112
    and Simpson Lever Chain, 44, 142
Gormully & Jeffrey, 152
Gougoltz, Jean,132–134, 136, 138–139
Grace, Clara, 143
Grand Prix International, 104

H

Hale, Teddy, 112
Harlequins Cricket and Football Club, 72, 90
    Sports Ground, 90
Haslingden, 10–11
Herne Hill track, 23, 109
Hofmann, Hans, 113
Honorary Artillery Company, 47–48
Hooly Ernest Terah, 42
Horton, A. W., 73
Hunt, George, 85, 87
Huret, Constant, 31, 44, 47, 52, 66–67, 78–79, 87–88, 91, 96, 111, 142, 146
    accident, 142

I

Ilsley, R. J., 110
industrial revolution, 7

International Cyclists' Association (ICA), 77
"Irish Brigade," the, 44

J

Jacquelin, Edmund, 96, 142, 146
Johnson, John S., 52, 120, 122, 161

K

Kennedy, J. C., 135
King's County Wheelers, 100
Kola Champagne, 64
kola nuts, 64
Kramer, Frank, 140

L

Laudanum, 63
le Gal, Amelie, (see also Marton,Lisette),118, 141–143, 148
League of American Wheelmen, 132
Leander, 138
Lesna, Lucien, 96, 122, 133
Linton Memorial Sports Day, 90
Linton, Arthur, 22, 32, 34, 44–45, 51, 68–92, 68–69, 71, 73, 75, 77, 79, 81, 83, 85, 87, 89, 91, 109, 112
and collapse and recovery in Paris–Bordeaux, 35, 85
and dispute with Warburton, 79
birth of, 71
declared Champion Cyclist of the World, 75
memorial, 90
mentor of Jimmy Michael, 109
sickness and death, 55–56, 88–92, 88
Linton, Samuel (Sam), 22, 71, 93–106, 109

and pacing skill, 94
birth of, 71
Linton, birth of, 70
Linton, Thomas (Tom), 22, 32, 40, 56, 70, 74–75, 78, 90, 93–106,130138
and accident, 106
and paced hour record, 96, 106
at Chain Races, 52
death of, 62, 106
move to America, 98
race against Jimmy Michael, 130
Lisette, (see le Gall, Amelie)
little black bottle
"Little Black Bottle," 61–67, 162
presumed contents of 36, 63
Luyten, Henri, 112

M

MacCabe, Dr. F. F., 44, 47–48
Madison Square Garden, 123, 136, 138, 153
maker's amateurs, 29–30
Manhattan Beach track, 99, 136
manufacturers, and maker's amateurs, 29–30
Marks, Dudley, 97–98, 101
Marton, Lisette (see le Gall, Amelie)
McDuffe, 122, 133, 140
McEachern, Archie, 136
McLeish, George S., 133
McNamara, Reggie, 140
McQuone, J. O., 38
Meyer, Charles, 78, 83–85
Michael, Jimmy, 22, 24, 29, 31–34, 43–45, 47–49, 53, 62, 57, 74–75, 78, 80, 82–83, 87–88, 96–97, 107–140, 142, 151, 161–162
and alcoholism, 137
and Berlin accident, 136
and break with Eck, 120
and death and funeral, 139–140
and disputes with and accusations

against Warburton 32–34, 53, 118–119
and disputes with Linton brothers and Warburton, 81, 116, 121, 127
and failure at Chain Races, 47–49, 62
and horse racing, 128, 134–136
and marriage and marital problems, 117, 127
and move to America, 118
and reburial, 139–140, 139
and training regimen, 115
and understatement of age, 119, 113
and U.S. citizenship, 127
and world championship title, 80
Michael, Willie, 127, 163
"Mighty Midget," as nickname for Jimmy Michael, 24
mixed-sex racing, 41
Morgan & Wright, 119, 128
motor-paced racing, and dangers of, 25, 31, 129, 148,
Muffaro, Joe, 153
Murphy, Charles "Mile-a-Minute," 126, 139–140
Mussabini165
Mussabini, Sam, and training methods, 53, 97, 164–167
death of, 167
hired to coach Dunlop pacing team, 53

N

National Cyclists Union (NCU), 8, 30, 39, 41, 53–54, 62, 143
and banning Albert Champion, 148
and enquiry of Michael's accusations against Warburton, 53–54, 62
mixed-sex racing, 41, 143
and road racing, 39

and maker's amateurs, 30
and women's racing, 41
National Track Association Team, 99
Neason, Billy, 85–87
Nelson, G. A., 82
Nelson, John, 136
Nieuport, Edouard, (see also Denieport), 56, 144–146
and aerodynamics, 145
and Warburton funeral, 146
Nightingale Hotel, 41
nitroglycerine, 63
North London Cycling and Athletic Grounds Ltd., 39

O

Oakley, Annie, 22–23
Osmond, F. J. "Freddy," 20–21
Oxborrow, Sansom, 112

P

paced racing, 20–21, 31, 43
Palmer, Dick, 114
Parc des Princes Vélodrome, 96, 134, 142, 148
Paris–Roubaix, 34, 82, 84, 95, 148
"Pittsburgh Girls," the, 154
Pivot chain, used in competition to Simpson Lever Chain, 48
Platt-Betts, 40, 44–45, 53, 82, 87
Polytechnic Cycling and Athletic Club, 38, 147, 166
Powell, Rev. M., 89
Powerbar, 63
Prince, John S (Jack), 152, 154–155
Prix Jimmy Michael, 140
Protin, Robert, 45, 87
Pure Water Company, 64

R

Reichel, Frantz, 45
Rivierre, Gaston, 34–35, 44, 83–87, 123
  and protest against Arthur Linton in Bordeaux–Paris, 86
Rutt, Walter, 113

S

Savoie, ocean liner, 138
Schwinn pacing team, 163
Schwinn, Frank, W. 139–140
Schwinn, Ignaz, 140, 161
Seine Vélodrome, 144
Shafer, Dave "Shiny Eye," 122–123, 128, 130, 133, 135
Shorland, Frank W., 73
Simpson, William Spears, 37, 43–47, 53, 58, 88, 91
Simpson Lever Chain, 37, 40–42, 84, 97, 143
Simpson Lever Chain Challenge (see also Chain Races), 44–45
Slater Jones, Dr., 58
Sloane, Tod, 128–129
Spoke, L. B. (see Bougle, Louis)
sports nutrition, modern-day use of, 66
St. Margaret's church, Aberaman, 90–91
Starbuck, Frank, 120, 133
stayer bicycle, 31, 147
steraculia, 64
Stocks, J. W., 33, 47, 51, 96, 114
Stone, Arthur, 130
strychnine, 63
Surrey Hundred, 23, 100, 109–110
Swindley, H. J., 38

T

Taylor, Major, 122, 132–133
Taylore, Edouard, 99–102, 105, 125–126, 133
Thé, Marius, 85–86, 106, 112
Titus, Fred, 100, 133
Toulouse-Lautrec, Henri, 43–52
  and Simpson Lever Chain poster, 45–48
  and Warburton image, 61

V

Vélodrome Buffalo, 32, 46
Vélodrome d'Hiver, 77, 143
Vélodrome de la Seine, 22, 46, 74
Vin-Kafra, 64

W

Wales, living conditions in, 68–71
  terrain' suitability for cycling, 69
Walter, "Jenny," 40, 44–45, 50, 56, 146–148, 151, 165
  and stayer bicycle design, 147
Walthour, Bobby, 136, 138
Warburton, James Edward ("Choppy") 9–18, 9–60, 61–67, 98, 141–150
  and lifestyle and dress style, 19, 24
  death of, 9, 58–60, 98
  and importance of rest, 36
  and inability to ride bicycle, 31
  and Jimmy Michael's accusation, 49
  and NCU ban, 54
  and initial move to Paris, 21
  and marriage to Mary Ann Johnson, 14
  and other riders, 141–150
  and initial problems with Jimmy Michael, 32

and sickness in Paris, 56
and training methods, 24–28
as runner, 9–18, 165
coaching career 19–54
compared to other trainers, 151
running career, 9–18
Warburton, James Allen (Jimmy), 14, 58, 102, 124
  birth of, 14
Water-Orton track, 20
Whittaker, Stillman G., 152
Williams, R., 87
Willow Grove Park track, 101, 123
women's racing, 40–41
Wood Green track, 38–39, 116

world championship titles before official championships, 75
world championship, first official, 32, 77, 112
"World Team," the, 162
Wridgeway, C. G., 47, 73, 110

Z

Zimmerman, Arthur Augustus, 45, 47, 52, 61
  as drawn by T-L, 61
  at chain races, 52
Zimmerman Prize, 144